OMINOUS OUTCOMES

A MATTHEW DIGGERSON MYSTERY

D.G. Gillespie

For information, email Cozy Cat Press at
cozycatpress@gmail.com
or visit our website at
www.cozycatpress.com

COZY CAT
PRESS

ISBN: 978-1-952579-14-1
Printed in the United States of America

10 9 8 7 6 5 4 3 2 1

Dedicated to my nieces Sarah and Elizabeth, who as children called me and Elena "Wesley and Buttercup." What greater compliment could anyone ever receive?

TABLE OF CONTENTS

CHAPTER ONE:

COURSE OUTCOMES

Any class—indeed, any learning situation—requires 'outcomes,' goals to strive for and reach, and in a writing class, those objectives call for a transfer of knowledge, the same as for any other field of study. Writing students need to know concepts (such as coherence), terminology (such as unity), tactics (such as focusing clearly), comparisons (such as logical versus illogical reasoning), etc., a more varied series of angles than for any other college course, especially since academic writers must turn that information into skills.

Suddenly, he was wide awake. In the pitch dark, the silence—a message, a warning to listen to. Could this be eternity? A coffin? *No*, too much like reality, like his brain doing its usual tricks, *the dark dance*. And darker lately, so much darker after his mother's abrupt illness and departure, almost as though she'd been poisoned. And she had, they all had. *They all had by dear old Dad!* His mother's coffin had been dark brown, and he knew that she had wanted a blond coffin; she'd told him that, away from his father, and he'd told the old man what she said. "Light," she had whispered. "Light wood." Still, *dark brown* it was, just like the hole she went into. The only human who'd ever really loved him. Just not enough, *not enough* to step in front of his father and all his abusive ways. Love was feeble, *not enough* to save a person or to give him a reason to be happy. *Not enough*, yet still she haunted him and always would. He saw that now, felt it in the dark, in the night's crystal hours when the stillness and silence drove out all pretense. His mother and her tattered love. Not enough.

He turned his head and saw that the bedside clock read 4:41. Almost 444, the number that announced an angelic presence, according to 'Ma,' but, of course, too early for that for him. Unlike his mother, he had many years to live, many paths to trod, an endless, loveless future. He groaned into the darkness, imagined the noise as a bubble that floated up and off. Even after looking away from the little Time machine, he saw the numbers burning, fiery red, imprinted on his eyelids. Didn't his clock have blue numbers? Time in his mind had always been blue, running inexorably like a river, but the river water was actually black, not blue. His sister, Beverly, she had given him this small clock, years ago actually, back when they'd been actual siblings, so now time was red. If he stared at the clock, he knew that the number wouldn't change, that Time would always win, make him flinch. He looked.

The clock now read 4:43. Time had lurched ahead, or maybe he'd been ruminating in the dark for two minutes. Time always did its thing even when you did nothing. Blazing away joys, sorrows, and boredom, burning red. Of course, Time was red because it burned everything in its wake to ashes. Hairlines and tight stomachs, goals and dreams. Mothers, not-enough mothers. It devoured the present and the past, too, the good and the bad; that only made sense. Yet some memories remained embers, never turned to ash, always glowing in the gloom. Like Beverly's absence at the funeral. *Imagine that!* Such tangible denial of the past, almost admirable. Utter erasing!

How his father had fumed at her failure to show last spring, how he had invented reasons for Bev's not being there, how his face had imploded a bit, embarrassment and anger wrestling and creating wrinkles and crevices, and had he not witnessed a touch of fear, too? A sheen of dread? The way the old man's eyes would dart to the horizon, checking to spot the arrival of his one and only daughter, his little princess, his Late Beverly. "Bevy!" his father had always called for her, and when she'd failed to respond to his summons, he'd look at his one-and-only son and say, "Where's your sister?" as though he had no name himself, as though he were hiding the princess. Maybe he should have. Maybe 'Bevy' had more reason than he did to move away from her past.

He lay in the dark staring at the red numbers, 4:43, picturing devils and waiting for angels, feeling his paunchy gut clench and jiggle. His mother had loved him, but not enough. Yet without her presence on the earth, the air was thinner, the landscape emptier, and what meaning could he find in the day's routine tasks? *Cleaning*, that was all. Cleaning was the meaning. Yes, erasing the dirt and the grime, not moving away from it but actually dealing with it, cleaning it up. Could meaning be found in action? That was his only hope.

Red numbers burning 4:43—stuck on that number. Time was playing with him again, being obstinate as usual, riding the silence, holding back, refusing to reach the future. Yes, to win against Time, a person had to act, to gather evidence, to plan, and then to be decisive. Goals were the one antidote to Time. When he closed his eyes, the darkness actually lightened a bit, so he kept them closed and thought about goals, checked each one off. One hit the bullseye; others fell off the board, false paths. Across his eyelids, '443' burned, refusing to turn.

What was darker and emptier than a New England cemetery in the night's lost hours? Void even of angels, the only presence was the past, and only here, in the graveyard, was that past alive. 'Personified' was the term. What was alive could be killed, that only made sense. *Erase and feel safe,* he thought, but when he tried to turn that little chorus into a tune, no song would come. *Oh, well!*

He rose up out of his car, the door croaking and squealing, *the rusty piece of crap!* He straightened up and listened. *Mother?* Nothing but *crickets* and other *bugs*. The unseen hoard of crickets was calling to each other, rubbing legs and screaming about Time because little of it for them was left. *Time!* It lay over this scene like a warm comforter, and for an instant he received the ironic image of snowfall, a thick coating. Just morning mist. *Smog!* He sniffed, the August air thick and a little sweet, heavy, as though this northern graveyard had been plunked down into New Orleans or some other god-awful sweaty place. He stopped his breath, and the same silence that held the crickets' calls in place bounced off of the bubble created around his head. He exhaled, and not even the crickets cared. *Just a bunch of bugs here.* His sister had always made a game out of driving past cemeteries, demanding that everyone hold their breaths until the stones were passed. *To keep the ghouls from swooping down your throat!* And, of course, he'd played along, just to make the little puke stop waving at the graveyard, her eyes wide, her cheeks puffed out. And, of course, their father would just ignore him and ruffle her hair, the little scamp. And when the last stone slid past, his sister would exhale loudly, with great fanfare, as though they'd just been saved. Another victory over death.

"Hold your breath," the living man said aloud to the dead, surveying the rising hillside and the pale, rectangular stones stretching up to the tree line far above. Apparently, all the residents were complying, even his mother, asleep on the hilltop.

He bent back into his little piece of *crap* car, pushed the driver's seat forward, and searched in back, rustling junk and papers. When again he straightened up, a yard-long sledge hammer hung from his hand close to the ground. Although he held the hammer closer to its base than its tip, the weight of the serious tool almost required two hands, but it felt good, meaningful. With his other hand, he tried to close the car door quietly, but it yelped a bit anyway, *the grumpy shit can!* He should buy another one, why not? Why save his money? He had plenty, had done well in his life, or not too *unwell*. And before too long, an inheritance, reparation. But the estate could wait, and he turned that thought into a little song, whispering it, imagining all the little crickets cocking their little black heads. This time, he decided, instead of some blue used piece of crap, he'd get a black car, maybe even a truck!

He thought about swinging the hammer into his current car a few times, but that was just a brain game. He had other plans in mind. A bead of sweat scurried down his temple and cheek and jumped from his head. *Like rats off a sinking ship.* But any ship would sink in this *August muck* for air. He hated the heat, but then he also despised the cold, the snows and winds that were always coming for New Englanders, an acceptance that was hammered into every Yankee's DNA, a branding at birth around these parts. A certain strength, a history, and nowhere else could a man better feel the past than in a New England graveyard. "Get on with it!" his father would have said, and that ghost of a voice reminded him of the great weight held, the sledge hammer, which wanted to feel the earth, to kiss a foe, anything, anyone. He thought of the wood and iron as an angry beast, full of malice, quite capable of fulfilling its bad intent, and by extension he adopted the same qualities. *Okay, Daddy!* Daddy wasn't talking anymore.

He looked up at the tombstones, rising in rows like movie-goers, some dark, some shining almost angelically. So many to say 'hello' to, so many *old friends*. All holding their breaths. At the top, his mother waited, and she had loved him. *Not enough!*

He began his ascent. First up, Tobias Mann. Birth date, end date. Almost twenty years, so this would be an anniversary of sorts for the old bastard. Amy Mann, just birth date. *She didn't want to join you, eh! Can't blame the old biddy.* Lying side by side with Tobias Mann for all eternity, *what punishment!* The hammer felt light now, ready, and he swung it as though he were reaching for a low pitch. Clunk. The stone didn't even shudder much. "Put some muscle into it," his father would have advised if the *old sonofabitch* could currently talk. Always plenty of that, fatherly advice, left over from the past. The son put some muscle into the next swing, which chipped the stone and made it wobble back once. More muscle, more wobble. More and a big crack, in the air and in the stone, which clonked over like a pair of trees, showing two rebars sticking out like bent cigars, long ones, *deluxe Tiparillos!* He moved behind the base and bashed the toppled stone halves a couple more times, cracking them into several smaller pieces. *Humpty Dumpty*, he thought. *Hard work! Cleaning with a hammer.* After several more swings, one per stone fragment, he moved up the hill, scanning the announced names, remembering where to go, for he'd visited before, many times lately, and memorized his current path. *Pinsky, Pinsky, where for art though, Pinsky?*

Daniel Pinsky. How formal! Now that he knew how to swing the hammer, this stone fell in just two whacks, and he left the broken halves alone this time, one declaring 'Daniel,' the other 'Pinsky.' *Poor, dumb bastard.* Next up, Pell, Pell, *the tolling of the Pells. Got to get them all from good old Ocean View College.*

Diana Pell. One big swipe this time, and *down she goes*, half of her anyway. The right-side rebar kept the 'Pell' side upright. *Okay, why not?* He'd show them how generous he could be. Plus, the hammer was growing heavier with each swing. Cleaning was hard work. He could hear his father now, calling him 'weak' and even worse than that. Too bad good old Dad's not in here, not yet, but maybe that would give away the game, and so much of the game was yet to be played. Up he walked, toward the top, where he dispensed two more stones, Valerie Walt and Johna Adams, just to create some intrigue. *John-uh*, he thought, *that's a weird name for a woman.* He tried to remember her, but no face came to mind, no memories. She couldn't have stood out much, yet connections were connections. It took five whacks to dispense of her gravestone because he was tired, his arms ached.

But strength returned for the next job: Eliot Gladstone. Irony. His 'stone' would not be 'glad' for long. With three great swings, he knocked the monument over and then took a couple half-hearted swipes at the word 'Eliot.' Sounded more like a girl's name. With each 'whack,' an echo would sweep down the hillside, quieting all the insects, and the man stood now in the silence, feeling the dragging pain to his right side. His right shoulder especially hurt, but the pain felt sort of good. The moonlight was shining on 'Gladstone,' and that made the man smile, a flicker of white, almost like a pair of lightning bugs meeting in the air. God, what *work!* Yet it had to be done, all this erasing. Symbolic actions, he knew, for he was not so uneducated that he didn't understand that nothing could really be erased, just like on hard drives. The pesky little files always remained in those dark corners, ready to be opened. But actions were the only choice, the only way out, his sole purpose now. Just one more stone to go tonight, and he gripped the sledge hammer right near its fat head and trudged a little higher up the hill.

But before finishing this first set of goals, he stopped at his mother's stone, which shone light grey, fresh. Time had not yet colored it with scabs of moss. He looked at her name and the years listed beneath it, as though those decades, those scattering of numbers, could possibly sum up a life. *Wives usually outlived their husbands*, he thought critically, but then his attitude softened. Over the years, his mother had enjoyed his quick visits home, always during the day when his father had been at work. "You know your father," she would always say and then imitate the man: "I'll work until the day I die!" Then she'd laughed, butterflies dancing in the air. He'd laughed with her, knowing that they both hated the man, feared him and admired him, too—yes, admired. The weak always admired the strong.

"Gotta go, Mom," the man quietly said to the grave and to the hilltop. "I've got one more stone to clean up. Can't leave the job half finished, right? Right." Then he tottered off, the sledgehammer dragging him to the right, throwing off his balance.

Diggerson, *good old Matty D*. During the planning, a month
ago, the son had been surprised to find this new stone atop the
hill, near his mother's, surprised and delighted, for it would be
the night's crowning achievement.   Right at the top, the
'crown,' near the newest additions, and there he was—they
were, the two of them. He moved around to the back, right up
against the forest that crested the hill, and in the wan
moonlight, he could read the legend carved into eternity:
'Listen, you can hear them sing.' He listened, couldn't hear
nothing! Just crickets. "Do you mean the crickets?" he said
aloud, and his voice sounded strange to him, and for a moment
the crickets stopped arguing. He listened again. Still *nothing.*
You're not singing very loud, he thought, but then he realized
why. *Of course,* he thought. *Nobody's home—yet!* A long way
to go. Each whack was just one check, one of many to mark
off, and he struck the new gravestone a vicious blow, which
blew it off its stand and cleaved it in two. *A home run swing!*
Right before the 'r' of Diggerson, he saw, with 'Matthew' on
one side and 'Anna' on the other. *The symbol of a broken heart,*
he thought, and in the dark, teeth shone palely in the
moonlight.

Then the crickets started screaming again.

Matthew Diggerson awoke suddenly, and immediately he
turned to find Anna but saw just an empty bed, dents and folds
in the pillow, the sheets. "Coffee!" he yodeled, but no echo
came, no Anna. Had she gone out already? When he checked
the digital clock, he saw that she probably had left, since it was
half past eight already and Anna was a morning person. Hadn't
she said something last night about shopping early? Digger had
mentioned that they needed eggs, and one of those Pepperidge

Farm coconut cakes, too. *Mmm, coconut cake!* He climbed out of the bed and walked sleepily to the kitchen. The coffee had been made! Where was Snodo? Bumper was probably out.

Digger sipped his coffee and went to the living room to find Snodo, who was fast asleep in her little oval dog bed beside the couch. The pet bed was new, for in the past Snodo hadn't needed it, springing like a goat onto the couch or onto their own bed. Now, though, Snodo was old and showing increasing signs of age. *Just like me*, thought Matthew Diggerson, looking down at his long-time companion, thinking how beautiful and sweet a sleeping dog looked. Partly, he'd slept late because every night, around 2 a.m. or so, he had to take Snodo out for a peeing. The old dog had begun to lose control, and she seemed so distraught with herself at those times that Digger vowed to help her from now on, so he slept a little later than usual because of those deep-night outings.

All through August, every night, when he awoke, Anna would, too, and she'd mumble something about "taking Snodo out" and then fall back asleep. Anna was a morning person, but not that early in the morning, not 2 a.m. early. On that last trip out, just a handful of hours ago, Digger had sensed autumn's whispering, the crickets calling for it, warning about it, and the wind had been tipped in a little chill. But perhaps that coolness had just been the ocean's breath, not fall's, not yet. Bumper had come with them last night, trailing after the man holding his dog, lowering the little animal, and holding the vertical leash taut while Snodo squatted. "Good girl," he'd say each time, and Snodo would look up at him with those big, deep eyes. "You're beautiful," he'd say to her in the lost hours of the night, beneath the stars.

According to his vet, Sarah Palmer, Digger had done the same thing with his lion dog, Simba, a decade earlier, but he could still remember nothing from that time, that lost year, due to the 22-caliber bullet that Eliot Gladstone, a long-time teaching colleague from Ocean View College, had fired into his head or perhaps to the ensuing long coma caused by the gunfire. Digger could not recall the shooting, which had occurred in his own living room, and when he'd finally awoken from the coma, he'd lost not only the violent incident, but the entire prior year. Gone were memories of people he'd met and even hired (he'd been the Humanities Department Chairperson at the time), of his classes (the students), even of the passing of his precious Simba, who had outlived her own mind. About her dementia, Digger had had to rely on information from Sarah.

"Snodo's old, Digger," Sarah had told him earlier in the summer. "She's just like Simba with all her pills and vitamins. It's just what you have to do."

As he sipped coffee, Digger tried to remember Simba's fall to compare it with Snodo's, which wasn't too bad, not yet, just a little sad. Snodo still had her mind, and Sarah had lamented more than once over the years how Simba had suffered from dementia. Funny how Sarah still talked about Simba, his mother, too. And he and Anna, who had never even known the Lion Dog, mentioned her often, usually when sitting out back. Thinking of Anna, he smiled, returned to the kitchen, and refilled his coffee. She was beautiful, too, and her surprise a few weeks back had made him want to both laugh and cry, so he'd laughed. A *tombstone!* They had a gravestone, how about that? Anna had done it all, had not even told him how much it cost, had just taken him to the Ocean View Cemetery and led him up the hill, saying that they should visit his father and sister, halfway up the hill, and then that they should view things from the apex. And there it had been—Diggerson, Matthew, Anna, and 'Listen, you can hear them sing' announced on the back side. Birth dates, too! He had goggled at it and then giggled, couldn't find words, and then he had laughed. "How? Why?" He couldn't even formulate questions, just kept staring at the stone and their names and the beautiful woodland scene below them, the fir trees, the moonlit grotto, where two dogs sat and two deer watched them from below the pines. It was really something, designed by his artist wife herself, of course, and every night when he took Snodo out and raised his head to the stars, Digger thought about that picture, about the 'Listen' on the back, about the sweet turn his life had taken, about 'everything under the sun being in tune,' with no 'eclipse' on the horizon, Pink Floyd, no, none at all.

Maybe just the shivery ripple cast by an aging white unicorn, maybe his mother, too, in her nineties at last, for how many people came out of that decade and into another? He sipped his coffee and decided to let Snodo sleep for a minute more. Out back, a troop of juncos landed, with their hooded grey cloaks and oyster-shell trousers. As a child, he'd called them 'snow birds,' a name that always followed 'juncos' in his mind and always made him think of his mother and their bird watching. The shadow of a memory, always clinging to any ray of light. That's how a person could stay grateful, through remembering, and Digger felt a great gratitude toward life, despite some shadows. *No, don't think of them, not yet,* not for another few months, maybe weeks, for however long the Shire dog had left.

Digger stared out the kitchen window. Why were the juncos here so early? Seeming to agree with him, a pair of blue jays crashed into the yard like uninvited guests, righteous and demanding, scattering the 'snow' birds. Digger thought of Labelia Baggins—had that been her name?—Bilbo's relative who always wanted Bag End. He would have to read Tolkien again, for imagine not being able to remember that name! Digger shaded his eyes against the slanting morning sun and looked for a third jay since those velociraptor-like birds seemed to come in trios. Maybe the third would be that one he'd seen years ago with the deformed crest, all dark and stubby, a scar that had separated him from the other jays. Checking the distant maples on the left and his fencing on the right, then the sky, Digger couldn't find a third blue jay and wondered if old stubby was still alive, still alone, still shunned by 'normal' jays. He raised his cup to Stubby and sipped again. *Oh, wonderful coffee!*

Time to get going. Digger pulled on a T-shirt, dragged up some sweats, and felt in the left pocket for a doggy 'waste' bag. *Check.* He liked to take Snodo for short walks, mainly because the little dog still loved them and partly to keep her nails short, for Snodo hated having them clipped. "Snodo," he called. "Snodo!" Bumper appeared—the Tom cat had been inside after all.

When Snodo staggered into the kitchen, looking sleepy and a little apologetic, white hair sprung out in all directions, Digger said, "Look at us staggering about, Snodo. What a pair!" The sound or maybe just the attention made the white dog's tail wave a few times, and it started moving again when Digger bent down and stroked Snodo's head. He clicked the leash to the harness, and they went out the back door. "Coming, Bumper?" The big cat seemed impervious to Time, continued every year to look fairly sleek and act slightly aloof and mysterious. Luckily, Anna seemed to have outgrown her cat allergies, for Bumper barely bothered her, even right after Anna had moved back in. Just a few sniffles and sneezes. Digger had said, "You're maturing," and his new old wife had given him that good-natured frown. How old was Bumper? Must be at least ten. Maybe more, but cats could live long lives, longer than dogs. Why was that? Usually, nature granted longer lives to the larger animals.

Snodo didn't want to traverse the porch steps, so as Digger carried the white bundle down, the ageless black cat moved off toward the beach. Bumper would jump on and over the gate, Digger knew, and then go exploring. Once, Digger had followed him, just to see where Bumper went, but the cat had caught on quickly and had just performed figure eights around the man's legs. Okay Bumper could have his secrets, like everyone.

Outside, the morning light from the beach colored the cottage's windows gold and made them look like rectangular Christmas gifts, sparkling. His only real neighbors, Graham and Donna, weren't around, and Digger wondered about Donna, whom he had not seen for weeks. He'd have to ask Graham about her. Graham! A good guy, but a bit of a dullard. Digger laughed at how Graham had thought that Anna looked "just like your old wife" as he'd said several years ago—and more than a few times since. Maybe he still didn't know.

Anna's little white car was gone, of course, just as Digger knew it would be, yet still that sight, that empty space, touched a sad spot, an echo of his black river, a place for doubts and angers. No, Anna would be back, with Pepperidge Farm cake, no less. Beside him, Snodo walked slowly, resolutely. At one time, she would have been pulling him like a sled dog, and more than once a stranger, a distant neighbor, had asked "Who's walking whom?" Probably, they'd left the 'm' off of 'whom,' *but who cares?* Now, just like this morning, Snodo usually hung back, more interested in sniffing than walking. Trying to make sense of the past, *like all of us.* At times, Digger found that he was almost dragging his little dog forward, so he'd learned to walk slower, to let her make the pace, just as before.

Snodo turned right down Cottage View Road and then left on a perpendicular little street called Rogers Lane, shaded and full of pot holes. Just before its end, at the main road to Ocean View College, where Digger had taught for three decades, the composition professor would always turn the little dog around and head back, but on this morning, the pair wouldn't get that far. Halfway down, both Digger and Snodo noticed two boys stomping on the ground and erupting in laughter and glee. Curious, Digger kept walking forward, and Snodo's tail began to wag. In the past, she would have barked long before now, but age had taken much of Snodo's voice.

The boys didn't notice them, even when Digger and his dog came within a dozen feet of the laughing pair. At his feet, Digger found multi-colored splats of orange and gold and realized that the boys were stomping on snails. Bewilderment erupted. These little explosions, pieces of the universe, lights from the heavens, dreams. These others, little gods, roaring and raging for no other reason than that they could, that they had the power, full of their own importance and need to display it.

Awakening, Digger said, "Why are you killing these snails?"

The gods, looking up, were mute, struck dumb. Caught in the act, frozen. They had become the snails, looked down upon.

Digger studied them, *pudgy* little humans. Were they suddenly scrutinizing their actions, finding themselves guilty, imposing silence as a penance?

"Where do you live? Are your parents home?"

At the reference to a higher power, the gods fled, released by a glance into the future, a flash of punishment, and that blush of importance, too, that small power, which they felt in their legs and their lungs as they escaped the man and his dog.

Snodo looked up at Digger, perhaps wondering if she should take chase, a possibility that fluttered through the man's mind. He remembered a Stephen King story, "Stand by Me," the main character's fear of dogs and of one in particular, the junkyard dog. 'Sick balls!' Digger smiled, giggled those four sounds: the first flat, then up a couple notes, down a bit, and back to flat. The odd little laughter was another 'gift,' along with the bullet, from Eliot Gladstone, erupting from the severed synapses of his brain and launching out whenever the writing teacher was amused or surprised, such as now. From the whooping escapees, Digger looked back at the shadowed ground. He was standing amidst a modernistic painting of splashed colors and no clear design. "No, Snodo," he said. "No 'sick balls' for you, and what would you do with 'balls' anyway?" The little unicorn looked up at him, her Mohawk stuck up and off to the side. When she cocked her head slightly, Digger laughed, and the dog's mouth popped open a bit. Sometimes, especially when she grinned, Snodo could look a lot like a hyena. At the top of the street, the boys had already disappeared.

At the opposite end—the mouth—far up from the desolation of the snails, a small car had stopped, blue, but Digger failed to notice it, his mind focused on the celestial splotches below, on the youthful yips and yups still bouncing around his head, on the incomprehensible creation that was humanity. *Wanton destruction.*

His mind on the earth, Digger saw that a few snails had survived on their trek across the hard grey sea of Rogers Lane, so with two fingers he gently plucked them up, one at a time, and tossed the snails into the foliage alongside the road as Snodo watched and sniffed. Up ahead, a couple more snails awaited salvation, and Digger thought of the worms on Ocean View College's rainy sidewalks. *OVC, worms, snails, wanton destruction.* These fleeing snails, their heads raised in effort, reminded Digger of some of OVC's worms, how they would wave one end about, most likely their heads, in an effort to cross the sidewalk. Often a futile effort. Nature could be cruel.

The blue car moved off just as Digger was turning Snodo back, having underhanded the remaining shelled creatures to the safety of soil and shade. He guided Snodo to the road's edge, not wanting to pass through the path of shattered snails. No doubt thinking of 'home,' Snodo moved ahead of him, and for a moment he recognized her old strut-trot of energy, which made Digger smile and reduced some of the bitter taste of the snails.

Out on Cottage Road, the blue car turned left down an adjoining street and then right onto the main road. Before long, it went left and then right into a fairly long driveway that ended at a low building announcing 'Breezy Seas Rehabilitation Center.' *Time for more scoping, more plans.* Diggerson was right: planning was fun. Gave the days a real purpose.

The blue car sputtered, and the man cursed. He hunched his shoulders, which still hurt. *Spirits' revenge.* He drove left at the

V-shaped building and turned off the piece of crap and got out. *Ouch!* He'd have to work out more or maybe just visit the cemetery more often. He could think of another stone that would soon need attention, or at least half of it. A pleasant thought, but even smiling hurt. He thought of his father's hypocrisy, falling ill within months as though he could no longer stand upright without his darling wife. Just more pretence, another façade, a lifetime built on appearances. He was more likely destroyed by Beverly's *betrayal*, as he no doubt had labeled it.

Above, white and puffy clouds sailed slowly south, dragging some tendrils of summer with them. Good! Take all the hot air away, yank it down south where they love that sort of thing, love sweating, like *pigs!* Pigs to the *slaughter*. He stood under the flickering sunshine and thought about pigs and about the old man dying down in Ward C, the sounds of breathing, the fat nurse scurrying around, the Spanish aide always creeping about. Have to keep an eye out for them, but that visit would be later. *One must stick to one's plans!*

"O-oh-o!" said Anna Cepatos, looking down at the sleeping man halfway down the corridor in Ward C. He had a hard face, prominent cheekbones and a long, downturned mouth, dark hair receding, dark eyebrows, the darkness touched by grey.

"A coma," said Nurse Addie, appearing in the door. "Old, but not so old as this."

Ana recognized the signs of coma, for she'd been an aide for ten years or close to it. Coma patients always looked so peaceful, both present and departed, but this man looked a bit more 'present' than most. *Cold.* Ana found herself wishing that he wouldn't wake up, at least not with her alone with him in this room.

"He's unlike our usual coma patients," said Nurse Addie. "Only sixty or so. So he might come out of this. The young ones often do. Remember our professor, the angel?"

"O-oh-o!" said Ana Cepatos, who for a decade couldn't erase the memory of Matthew Diggerson and his pale angel, how he'd slept so beautifully, how he'd awoken so magically, how the beautiful woman with her own first name had spirited him away in the night. Ana often thought about her sleeping prince and his princess, the nice woman with the long, light hair, the green eyes that would turn blue in the shadows. Where were they now? In what castle? Ana's life had narrowed to Breezy Seas and to her own family, and the years had brought constant change to everyone but her. Long ago, Margrita, the chubby older aide who had helped Ana so much, had announced her departure with "I've cleaned enough people's crap," and a year or so later, Julio, the skinny younger aide who hadn't helped Ana so much, had punctuated his final day with "Had enough of people's crap!" *People's crap* seemed to be the Breezy Seas' theme, but in the most extreme of realistic worlds, Ana Cepatos had maintained her innocence. She still found wonder in these old, old lives, and many of the bed-ridden souls—the ones who were conscious—spoke to her about their pasts, their triumphs and regrets. They seemed to find solace in the introverted aide, and Ana found something in them, too, even when they made little sense.

She and Nurse Addie stood looking at the sleeping man. "Well," said the older woman, "no time to stand here and gawk. We all have our work to do." Ana nodded and resumed cleaning the little room, alone now, but her chores took longer than usual because she feared to turn her back on the cold man, whose dreams seemed troubled and unappealing, whose closed eyelids seemed ready to snap open.

CHAPTER TWO

THE PURPOSE OUTCOME

Perhaps the single most important element to any writing assignment, the 'purpose' represents the writer's reason for writing in the first place. If a student fails to follow a professor's *purpose*, then he or she dooms the paper to fail. For instance, if the purpose is to summarize and the student analyzes, or vice versa, then the teacher learns not only that the student cannot follow directions, but also that he or she lacks the skill to summarize or evaluate. Writers must always know their purpose, which for 95% of college assignments is to 'explain.'

"What song's in your head?" Anna was smiling, holding his coffee, which was steaming. With that grin, she must have quite the tune in mind.

"'Hallelujah,' Leonard Cohen, the perfect morning melody," he said. "Umm, thanks for the coffee."

"You didn't even have to call for it, either. But don't you want to know the song in my mind?" she asked. "It's 'Round and Round,' by Ratt!"

"With that song banging through your head, you don't even need coffee."

"'What comes around goes around,'" Anna sang, and Digger giggled.

"Can't argue with Ratt," he said, the lyrical chorus taking him back to Eliot Gladstone, to Paul Smith.

His wife must have caught these dark musings, for she grew serious, her forehead forming a 'V.' "It's even true with those toppled gravestones, Matt. 'What comes around goes around.' Why those stones? Why Tobias Mann's and Diana Pell's, and those two women who were killed, and ours. Why ours? What's 'coming around' now?"

"I might need more coffee for this conversation," said Digger, "but let's see. The cop said that it was probably some *nut* who'd followed all those old murders and who just went around smashing the names that had been in the articles. Could have been teenagers, Anna, probably was. Teens can read, they just don't want to. Anyway, the police don't seem to take the vandalism very seriously. The cop wasn't worried. He said that the person or people probably didn't even notice that we weren't under our own stone, that ours had no death dates."

"You don't feel in any danger at work, do you? I certainly don't know anyone at OVC who seems to dislike me, or you, for that matter." Anna had taught as an adjunct professor at Ocean View College for the past several years, ever since reuniting with Digger.

"You know, Anna, it's hard to tell. My *colleagues*. I thought Paul Smith was odd; I used to call him and his wife the Morbids, but I never thought he could kill anyone. Same for Eliot Gladstone, or as you'd call him 'Professor Happy Rock.' He could be strange, but I never would have branded him a killer."

"Any 'strange' or 'odd' colleagues left? Who comes to mind immediately?"

"Well, maybe Lou Knightly, but I'm not sure why. He's not negative like Paul or Eliot, and maybe it's just his constant lip licking that seems odd. Yet Lou's the only one who ever talks about my books, asks about them. He's even read a couple, I think. He seems to know about Billy D. Wilder and some of my plots, at least for the first two books. And now that he's newly married, he'd seem too preoccupied to go bashing through a graveyard." Digger paused. "Basically nobody else ever says a thing, even though my protagonist is a college writing teacher, just like them, and even though the setting's a fictional Ocean View College, just like where they work."

"I've heard colleagues mentioning your book, Matt. Sometimes someone will ask me what it's like being married to an author? The art teachers all love the idea of a partner who writes a lot and leaves them alone to do their own art."

"We balance it well, don't we? But going back to your question, you know the first name that came to mind, just a flash before Lou, was our resident lesbian, Jolie, and it's not her being gay that's odd, it's her mannerism. She's always ready for a fight, it seems. Shields up, weapons locked. Jolie always seems just a little bit angry."

"Where did she go to school?"

"The University of Rhode Island, but why do you ask? Do you think that all Rhode Island Rams are angry homosexuals?"

"That sounds like a rock band, Matt, or punk rock, 'The Angry Homosexuals.' But no, I was just wondering. That's the question all my art colleagues always ask. Where did you go to school? And what did you study? And why are people always trying to kill your husband. No, just kidding. Not that last question."

Digger giggled, said, "You know, my colleagues are the same. The same questions, college and field of study, and I'm guilty, too. I wonder if we're all just trying to categorize each other, put each other into safe places, safe for us."

In the silence following Digger's indirect question, Snodo walked into the kitchen, looked up at them, wagged her tail softly, and then sank down between the two humans, butt first. For a year, at least, Snodo had been less energetic, almost matching Bumper's sedate speed now, and in late August she'd slipped going down the wooden porch stairs and even had trouble climbing them at times. Although she was on anti-inflammatory and pain pills—one each, the hairy white dog still enjoyed life and food, still had that spark in her eyes, a glint that both beamed out and disappeared far down into the light mahogany richness, the gold glitter. How could something no larger than a big marble hold so much light, so much life?

"I'll never forget when Snodo first saw you at Breezy Seas. Do you remember how crazy she was, Matt? Like a rocket bouncing around, and then how she slumped down on your bed and just stared at you with those giant eyes."

"Her basset hound genes, I think," Digger said, and then he added that Snodo's always looked at Anna the same way.

"She sure knows how to love."

"Loyalty and faith, respect," summed up Digger. "Dogs are the real teachers."

Each human thought of the other, measured themselves against canine love. They had been married (again) for eight years now, repeating their vows the summer after Digger's reawakening and just a few months after Eliot Gladstone had forced Digger to walk the plank but then plunged into the depths himself. The golden glow of the past eight years had sewed together the wound left by Anna's departure long ago, and nothing of that solitude remained in Digger's conscious thoughts, perhaps just a hint hovering above the black river that flowed below, a mist riding the breath of that dark stream, perhaps best classified as the unconscious. He delved into that black stream now, dipped down to look for shadows, for grave topplers.

He thought of Bill Jacobs, of the obituary in their local paper last month, and Gemma Jacobs, Bill's wife. Lou found a wife, Bill lost one. Digger remembered the words "after a long illness" and wondered if Gemma Jacobs' gravestone had been smashed, too. But probably she'd had no stone yet. Few people were like him and Anna, thinking ahead and fixing up their own final little home on the hilltop. When had Digger last seen Bill? A decade ago? *Why was everything 'a decade ago'?* Of course, although Bill could've kept in contact with Digger, it was no surprise that an adjunct would just disappear, especially since OVC made no fuss over their departures, their connections for years and years, and then their disconnections. No gold watches, not even any announcements. Nevertheless, Digger felt guilt prickle, for he could've stayed in contact with Bill Jacobs. He wondered if Bill's Gemma had inhaled her last breath at home or from a small beeping room at Breezy Seas or one of its sisters. *Chinese boxes, that's where we live,* Digger thought to himself, *and Time keeps switching us from a bigger box to one that's a little smaller, then smaller, then our final box, of course, the one that's hidden beneath the earth.*

"You know that I want to be cremated?" he said, but Anna ignored the remark. She was Catholic, perhaps not rigidly so, but some rules just could not be broken.

Digger laughed. "Cremated!" he said and laughed again at Anna's frown. She'd heard him, all right. He sipped his coffee and looked down at Snodo, sleeping already, her white hair sticking out in all directions, as though an explosion had occurred inside. No cremation for the white beagle, she'd lie with Simba out back, in the cool, sandy soil. And soon Snodo would need to go outside, as soon as she woke up.

Anna cut into his reveries. "The cemetery guy said that our stone will look as good as new, in about a month, and that it won't cost anything, that their insurance will cover everything." Then she laughed. "He kept calling it *your parents' stone.* He just couldn't get it through his head that we had one for ourselves already."

"You didn't have to set it all up, Anna, but I'm glad that you did, even after what happened—the vandalism."

"The guy said that we were 'lucky,' that *your parents' stone* had a clean break.' He said that Tobias Mann's was smashed into a 'million pieces, a total loss.'"

Digger wondered about that, about someone who hated Tobias Mann so much that he'd pulverize his gravestone nearly two decades after the haughty fellow had entered it. Hatred, anger, revenge: just some of the sinuous currents from his or anyone's black river. Paul Smith? Was Mr. Morbid even alive still? Could he have been released from prison, a two-time murderer? *No, impossible,* and Paul's motivation had been, what, despair? Eliot's had been jealousy, Paul's despair, and now anger, maybe bitterness, or maybe just a group of teenagers who'd read an old article and decided on a little spooky fun.

"Even the back of the stone will be fine," continued Anna. "The break occurred right after the word 'Listen.'"

"Right where the pause should come; right before 'you can hear them sing.'"

"I'm surprised that you allowed that run-on, Matt, that you didn't want a semicolon or colon after 'Listen.'"

"Not all us writing teachers are so pedantic, my wife, and sometimes good writing means bending rules, depending on genre."

Anna looked pensive. "Eliot's stone was smashed, too, yet maybe that was what you'd call a, what? 'Red herring,'? Isn't that the term? A wrong path? Wasn't Eliot jealous of your books? Isn't that why he tried to kill you?"

Despite that dark truth, Digger giggled. "Are you saying that he came back from the grave for another shot?"

"What grave?" said Anna seriously. "His body was never found, right? Maybe he popped up somewhere and his brother ferreted him away."

"Now you sound like my mother, always worrying about things that'll never happen. Eliot's gone, Anna. I saw him go down; I saw the currents. You've seen the Whirlpool, you know."

"I know, I know. I'm just brainstorming, as you'd say. But let's throw out some more thoughts, about jealousy, about your books. You've been the Guest Author at the library how many times—three? Who showed up in the crowd, besides me, of course? Any of your colleagues?"

Digger felt his black river gurgle, a small black belch. "No."

"What about that librarian, the Mystery Club lady who set up your visits, Bonnie Something, right? Maybe she's not so 'bonny.'"

Digger giggled again. "Nobody named 'Bonnie' could be a killer, or even a grave toppler. That takes muscle. You remember what Bonnie looks like; can you see her with a sledge hammer in one hand and a pry bar in the other?"

"Just brainstorming, Matt, just ideas. I never actually thought about how the person had knocked over the gravestones. I guess it must have been a sledge hammer. What's a 'pry bar'?"

"You know, a long stick of iron, with a wedge on one end. I have one in the garage, but I never really use it. They're good for yanking stones out of the ground."

"That's just what the person did, too, at the cemetery."

"It's like the person wanted to kill the dead again."

They paused to consider that oxymoron. Then Anna smiled and said, "You don't have to worry about that, Matt. You're an author, you'll never really die."

Digger smiled, but his thoughts below his lips turned dark, for later that week he'd start the fall semester and see his colleagues. His *friends*. An author who isn't read—wasn't that like a tree falling in the woods with nobody noticing?

"Sometimes, Anna, I feel a little dead already." Then he added quickly, seeing her mouth pout, "Oh, not with you, not here, Anna, not with you in the cottage. You and Snodo and Bumper, and I almost said 'Simba,' too."

Anna gave him a sad smile, for she knew his mind, his joys and sorrows. "Go ahead and say 'Simba; she's still here, and she'll be here as long as you are, maybe forever since she's in your books, right? You've made her immortal, Matt. Both you and Simba are immortal."

"If we are, then you too, Anna, because you know about Billy D's biggest regret, about Lana, the one he let get away, the one that haunts him in all of my books. All I had to do was think of what life would have been like if we'd split long ago, before we ever really formed. You're in every story, Anna, all four. And your paintings are just like my writing. They will live on, so you will, too."

Anna laughed. "We're immortal! It feels good."

"Immortal," repeated Digger. "Maybe so; maybe I finally found a way to beat Time, that sonofabitch!"

The two humans laughed, the real way to beat Time: by being happy. When they heard a small groan at their feet, Digger and Anna looked down and saw that Snodo's paws, all four, were twitching continually, as though she were dog paddling through the air.

"Snodo, Snodo, are you ready to go out?" said Digger, but the white dog was far away, running younger and upright in the land of dreams.

On Wednesday, the first day of Digger's fall classes, the writing teacher sat alone in his office and thought again of dreams, for the Dream Board was gone, leaving a three-foot square pale spot on the wall outside his little room. At the summer meeting, hosted now by Lou Knightly, the department chairperson for the last few years, Digger had noticed that the Dream Board (which he'd set up a decade past to highlight faculty writing) had grown old, brittle, and forgotten, and now it was just gone. Lou hadn't even mentioned ordering the board to be removed. No doubt, George North, still the Faculty Office Building janitor the past several years, had disposed of it, jammed it into the trash bin out back, probably. *A sad end for dreams*, but Digger still had his. Four books now: *Composition Murder, Murderous Mistakes, Perilous Persuasion,* and *Ominous Organizations*. Gloria, the department secretary, had read them all, and Lou, the Lip Licker, had mentioned details about the first two. In fact, only Gloria and Lou, the closest thing Digger had to a friend at OVC, ever said anything about his books. Over the years, Digger had given up mentioning anything about them or about writing them to anyone else since the others' lack of reaction, of interest, was so disappointing, even alienating, especially as he sat alone in his office during office hours. He would no doubt have a semester full of those this fall, email having done in office hours.

Across the hallway, the door was closed. Lou's office now. Digger drifted back to picture its former occupant, Diana Pell, the poet and reluctant smiler. She would have been long retired by now and should be sitting at a desk at home, sipping coffee (or probably tea), scribbling lines as snowflakes drifted down unseen out the window, lines of verse trying to make sense of the rock-filled path called life. Digger focused on the imagined snowflakes, on weather that he enjoyed more than September's still often sweaty days.

Where was Lou? At home in wedded bliss? Shouldn't the Chair be available for students who wanted to escape hard-grading teachers or to join classes containing their newfound friends? For that matter, shouldn't the Chair order a case to be installed to showcase faculty publications, such as four murder mysteries? The business building contained a display case of faculty publications, head high, five shelves, and the science people had one, too, two of them, in fact. Yet the Writing Department had nothing but a history of killers and corpses. *Killers and Corpses.* Digger thought of what Anna had said about a band's name that morning, something about 'homosexuals.' Killers and Corpses sounded like a heavy metal band's name. He could call her and mention the name, but Anna probably wouldn't be home yet. She sometimes shopped after school, too. *She buys, I cook,* thought Digger, not a bad setup. Then he imagined a display case. No, Digger wouldn't even bother, for Lou would just mention the cost, blaming administrators.

Where was everyone? Probably teaching, getting ready to wrap up classes. Soon the hallway would echo with sound, and Digger looked forward to it. He liked and even needed camaraderie, craving it, even if the connections were thin and superficial, weather talk, for instance. Offices could be very lonely. And, of course, Digger wanted to keep his eye out for any smirking peers, anyone with a rock-tumbling glint in their eyes. What would that look like? A flicker of orange, perhaps, fire. Wasn't that Eliot Gladstone's book, something about 'fire'? Maybe William Watkins, Dr. Psycho, would know how such malice would look, but he'd finally retired. OVC had put up a stout bench in his honor beneath a maple tree alongside the Psychology Building, so now anyone could sit on Watkins at last. That made Digger smile. About his peers' lack of interest in Digger's written efforts, Watkins had once said, "Maybe they just don't like you." or something like that. Odd how a statement could stick to a man's thoughts, stay hooked in the brain for years, like a little bullet.

Class soon. Digger should start to get ready, but he knew what to do, wasn't worried. Then he heard footsteps and got up to investigate. Jolie, dressed a bit informally as usual—T-shirt and slacks.

"Here we go again, Digger," the approaching woman said. His colleagues all called him 'Digger,' as though they were all close, connected by nicknames. Digger had once told Anna that "when your name's 'Diggerson,' you're going to be called 'Digger,' and you hear all sort of jokes about grave digging." But what else would they call him?

Digger smiled and they traded schedules, the typical talk, schedules and weather. Digger asked about Jolie's partner, Mary, and the conversation went like this:

Jolie: "Two years already. Better than most marriages!"

Digger: "Two years is a good start."

Jolie: "We're more monogamous than people think." Digger wondered if by 'we' she meant lesbians in general or she and Mary in particular, but he dropped that thought. Anna's band name drifted through his mind.

Digger: "You got the last Mary."

Jolie: "The last Mary? What do you mean by that?"

Digger: "Nobody names their daughters 'Mary' anymore. I haven't had a student named Mary in twenty years."

Jolie: "That could be taken another way, you know, Digger. The last Mary."

Digger: "What other way? I don't follow you, Jolie."

Jolie: "Marys, you know, Marys! Bigots call gay boys, or boys with feminine mannerisms, 'Marys.'"

Digger: "That's right; I forgot. Sort of before our time, though, wasn't that term? Even before mine."

Jolie: "Bigots are timeless. The last Mary, that sounds like a Republican's dream, doesn't it? Are you a Republican, Digger?"

Digger: "No, but you sound a little like Diana Pell; she used to complain about Republicans; remember?"

Jolie: "Oh, I've lived a life of political complaints; my father and all of his Democratic conspiracies. *Anything* could be blamed on a Democrat, even my own sexual preferences." She laughed, then frowned. "I can hardly remember her now, Digger—Diana, that is."

Digger: "I tend to hang onto loss longer than most, I think. But isn't the 'last' of anything sort of poignant? My mother currently has just one cat, a very old one, too, and it's her *last* one, she says."

Jolie: "The last lemming, think of that,—those rodents that commit mass suicide by jumping off cliffs, one after another. What does the last one think, the last lemming, all alone? All the others have scrambled over the cliff, so doesn't the *last* one want to stop and reassess the situation, decide not to be a follower?"

Digger: "Maybe it thinks there's something better on the other side, or it just wants to be part of the group. Maybe the sacrifice is worth it."

Jolie: "Or maybe it's just a dumb rat, Diggerson. Sounds a lot like my brother."

Digger ignored the comments, noting that Jolie was more prickly than usual even, and then empathizing with her sibling, whom he'd never met or perhaps never even heard of. This conversation had already progressed twice as long as any he'd ever had with this peer, and Digger realized that Jolie's statements sounded like E chords, for she declared things—powerful and assured. In contrast, Anna's spoken sentences rang out more like G chords, interested, excited even. What notes did Digger make? Probably A-minors, maybe common C chords?

"The Last Lemming," he said. "It sounds like a song or maybe a poem. You should write another song, Jolie. 'The Last Lemming' or maybe 'The Last Mary.' You could get all sorts of imagery and symbolism into it."

"*You* write it then, take my lemming idea and turn it into one of your murder mysteries. I can't. My musical talents have all dried up. Diana would hear that and say, 'Like a raisin in the sun,' wouldn't she? I do remember her."

Digger thought of dreams 'deferred' and then suddenly of Eliot Gladstone, his terminal jealousy of the great writer David Ross Winslow, the way that sickly green emotion ate away at him, from the depths, gangrene.

"Get it going again, Jolie, the music. We all need to sing."

After going back to his office, Digger thought about Jolie, one of those people, like Madonna or LeBron, who didn't need a last name, and it took him a few seconds to conjure up his colleague's: *Matterson*. He had heard students asking for 'Professor Matterson,' but Digger had never uttered that name himself. *Sounded a bit like his*. He pictured her holding a sledge hammer; just couldn't see it. Their conversation had been long, much longer than his usual colleague connections, and had contained some substance. He knew about lemmings, of course, had just pretended that Jolie was telling him something new, yet he had enjoyed the communication. *You take what you can get*. It was time to *get* going, time to begin the fall semester.

Digger's schedule had been just about the same for over a decade, even longer: late mornings/early afternoons on Mondays, Wednesdays, and Fridays, with Tuesdays and Thursdays 'off'—from classes, anyway. In the fall, he taught EN 101, 'Freshmen Composition,' probably the most feared and disliked college course in American history, and definitely the most important, at least within students' first two years, before they really delved into their major's workload. Although four classes in five hours took some effort, Digger loved the 'space in time' that this schedule offered, a day at least between each class day, as well as more time at home twice during the week.

All four classes looked promising this semester, none of the students' seeming too disengaged (too stuck to their cell phones!), all appearing to enjoy the collaborative introductions exercise that Digger did on the first day each semester, an ice-breaking activity that he'd read about from some business article on effective presentations. Digger had simply changed the workplace questions a bit and had students work in groups of four, sometimes three, interviewing and introducing each other.

After the last class ended, at close to four, Digger left the Classroom Building to fulfill another sixty-minute office-hour obligation and saw his quiet colleague, Jeff, leaving the FOB (Faculty Office Building) and heading off toward the Faculty Parking Lot. Digger waved but then experienced that silly feeling when the other person didn't see him and failed to return the effort. Since Jeff's office was up the hallway from Digger's and they always seemed to be on different schedules, Digger never saw much of the reclusive, scholarly Jeff. Just at meetings really. Jeff always spoke very deliberately, very diplomatically, as though never wanting to ruffle any feathers, to create any wind at all. He seemed very knowledgeable and capable, one of those people whom others simply took for granted. Digger couldn't even remember listing him as a suspect in past murder investigations. Well, if Jeff were around this time of day *this* semester, perhaps Digger could communicate with him a bit, make a connection. Digger thought of his books, pictured again Jeff's scurrying off. *Probably no connection.* Then he thought of Jeff's lugging around a sledge hammer—*not a fit.*

Then Lou Knightly popped out of the FOB, and Digger giggled, thinking of a Pez dispenser. Lou saw him and waved, waited.

"There's the married man!" said Digger. "Why aren't you hurrying home?"

"Oh, I am, Digger. I am. Just lots of stuff to do, you know how it is, being the Chair, lots of crap, that's what most of it is."

"Moving students from one section to another, that sort of thing. I remember well and miss it not at all! Students all want to get into their friends' classes, right?"

"Oh, yeah, and why can't they just say that, Digger? Why do they make up stories about hearing of this wonderful teacher and wanting to get into their class? Or they have family obligations and thus need a later class time."

"Family emergencies!" laughed Digger. "But seriously, how's married life? How do you like living with someone? What's your wife's name again?"

Lou said that it was "Angela" and that he liked it, but Digger noticed a continuous passage of tongue over lip, something he'd connected to the man's anxiety level. Or maybe he was just imagining things.

"How about your in-laws?" Digger asked. "Any problems there?"

"None," said Lou, adding, "They live in California!"

Both men laughed loudly, startling a chickadee, who then began to hoot at them.

"Look," said Digger. "A chickadee already, in September?"

"The real problem's my father," said Lou, ignoring the chickadee and its self-proclaimed complaints. "He didn't want me to get married, the old bastard. I think that he wanted me to take care of him in his dotage. He's not doing so well."

"I'm sorry to hear that, and your mother? I forgot if she's still alive, Lou."

"No, no, she passed, years ago," said Lou Knightly, his boxy head angled toward the pavement, looking down on Matthew Diggerson. Then the tall man barked a laugh. "She probably wanted to get away from my father, but here he comes again, Digger. Watch out, Mom!"

Digger wasn't sure how to respond to this joke, if that's what it was. Amongst his colleagues, 'fathers' seemed to be a touchy topic. Since 'the other half' appeared safe, he said, "My mother's still alive, and she will happily tell you that she's ninety years old. She can be a handful, too."

"Ninety! Wow. My mother was far younger, and my father's not that old, either, but he's always been a little rotten inside. That's just honesty, Digger. Maybe he'll change, right?"

"Nobody changes," said Digger without thinking first, for his mood had been affected. Where was that chickadee? Gone.

After Lou left, Digger ascended the two flights of stairs, thinking of his own father, gone for so long that his voice no longer even rang in Digger's memories, and turned down the Humanities Hallway, the scene of two past murders. The darkened passage often frightened the composition teacher just a little bit, just a couple of prickles, perhaps several, especially when it was so quiet, as it almost always was at four in the afternoon with all the doors closed. Gloria Swanson, whose secretarial desk took up much of the alcove and turned her into a gatekeeper of sorts, tended to leave by 3:30. After Lou, Digger could have used her smile, a small connection.

As he approached the adjuncts' communal office, Digger remembered what Bill Jacobs, the curmudgeon, the long-time part-timer, the recent 'widow,' had said to him, that Digger had been the only full-timer who ever entered that closet-like, windowless room to connect with the adjuncts (the "hoi polio," Bill had said), and those words had always stayed with him, haunting him, even motivating him to stop and say hello to various part-timers, at least once a week. Certainly, with shared committees and continuously changing university policies and responsibilities, Digger and his fellow full-timers had more topics to discuss. But both sides resided in the same discourse community, shared the most important goal, to teach students how to write better, so why not stop and communicate? If for no other reason than simple humanity, simply sharing interest and offering camaraderie, Digger was motivated to visit the drab office where he'd once looked out at the passing world of royalty, the full-timers' progression.

The door was closed, and no noise followed Digger's knock. Usually, he found a couple part-timers in this room, and new people came with every fall semester. Lou Knightly had hired a man and a woman, and Digger thought of the pair and of the need for another full-timer or two, too. *Adjuncts in, adjuncts out,* he contemplated. The department's breathing. One whom Digger had hired, Jay Moore, the Blinker, had never left and still taught both day and night classes. Too early for him to come for a night class, though; too early for anyone. No adjuncts had been converted to full-time status since before Digger's being chair due to a campus hiring freeze. Part-timers saved the school major dollars, not only in salary, but in reduced health-care costs since adjuncts were not part of the 'free' benefits awarded to all full-time faculty and staff. For that reason, across all of higher education, introductory courses were staffed by part-timers and graduate students. At OVC and elsewhere, the school would occasionally post full-time positions, as required by law, but hire from 'in house,' mainly to keep a talented adjunct and to foster hope in all the others. The golden carrot!

Every summer, adjunct faculty were added, just as Digger had once hired Jay and the murdered woman whom he could not remember, yet whose name he could not forget. Johna Adams. The two latest adjuncts were a fairly young guy named Ben something, *Ben Bodine*, who'd already described his own unpublished writing to Digger without once asking about any of Digger's four *published* mysteries, and Elizabeth George, who'd said to Digger after the summer meeting that "mysteries were not my *genre*," accenting the last word as though it had a scent. Digger had laughed because, of course, 'Elizabeth George' was the name of a famous mystery writer. "With your name," he'd responded, "you'd either love or hate murder mysteries, right?" But the somewhat young woman who seemed older had simply said, "Too prescriptive."

Digger smiled at the memory, unlocked his office, gazing first at the empty pale space that once displayed the Dream Board, and sat at his desk. He called home, but Anna didn't answer. He looked out the narrow window and saw the clock towers' shadows. Both clocks offered the same time, surprisingly, and Digger was happy to see that his conversation with Lou had eaten into his office hour a bit. A gull swooped by the window, startling the seated man, who after another half hour or so decided to skip out ten minutes early.

He was caught by the janitor, who always seemed to know what was going on and to be compelled to announce it.

"Leaving early, eh!" said George North, one arm wrapped around a mop, as usual. Digger no longer thought of George as a former student, not often; now, he was simply the janitor. Time had made that change. Others, as well, for George was becoming more like the old custodian, Dan Pinsky, just not with all the booming 'Lord' talk. George apparently had no spirit guides.

"You know how it is, first day, George. Nobody really wants to start, not the students, anyway. How are you?"

"Can't complain," said George, who must have been thirty-five, thought Digger, but who looked older than that, mainly due to his receding hairline, the slight paunch, and the beginnings of jowls.

"But everyone still does, right?"

"Oh, yeah," said George, and his mop went back and forth twice, then stopped. "Especially my father, always complaining." *Fathers again?* "Not about me for a change, though," continued the maintenance engineer. "This time about himself."

"That's a nice change then, right?" Digger started to move away. He didn't really want to talk to George about his father. Too much *father bashing*, especially when he'd gone without his own for most of his life, it seemed. "I'll see you Friday, George," he said, and the old/young man responded in kind. George would no doubt be alone in the FOB now, and Digger wondered if he enjoyed that time.

On the sidewalk outside the Administration Building, Digger discovered a pair of worms trying to traverse the cruel, grey sea of the concrete sidewalk, and he thought of snails, of gleeful children. Usually, the worms appeared in the mornings after nighttime downpours, but apparently it had showered at some point while Digger was inside. He stared at the pair of worms. Were they together? *Fellow travelers.* Husband and wife. Father and mother. Without even checking for human onlookers, he bent down and helped the thin creatures complete their journey. The sidewalk ahead looked free. Late afternoon at OVC was a somewhat empty time, and Digger passed only a couple of students as he walked. They exchanged *hellos* each time, for everyone was full of happiness and hope at a semester's beginning. Later on, during the long month of October and beneath November's winds, people would walk downcast and simply ignore any passersby. Thinking of the end, trying to reach it.

Approaching the faculty parking lot, Digger encountered another wiggling worm, its head (or tail) wagging away, just a brush of pink on that end. A 'handsome' worm if that word could be used on such a creature. When Digger bent down and reached for it, the little fellow began to spasm, its entire body flopping about in sections, like a furry dog shaking off water. "Just trying to help," Digger whispered as the grey string wiggled, and then he thought of a joke: one worm squiggles up to another and says, "My ass looks like your face!" Digger giggled, scooped up the frightened worm, and slow tossed it into the dirt beneath a nearby bush. "There you go," he communicated in silence, then continuing on his wormless way.

Driving home, he thought of his joke, deciding to flip it around for Anna so that the final word was the strong 'ass,' not the weaker 'face.' *Your face looks like my ass!* Then he decided that the joke was too quick, over before Anna would even know that it had begun. He realized that some things needed to be 'set up,' planned, and with that thought in mind, his joke faded out, replaced by the image of white slabs rising up a hillside, a graveyard, cloaked in the dead of night. Was someone planning something? Were unseen dominoes about to fall? Like gravestones.

CHAPTER THREE:

THE STEPS OUTCOME

Writing requires a series of steps, the major stages being generating ideas, planning topics, researching, writing, revising, and editing, but each of those areas could also be broken into sub-steps, such as editing into checking for weak-verb wordiness, reading aloud to hear errors, using the Ctrl/F computer search for issues, and even going to another person for proofreading help. Think, too, of how each of those sub-steps could be narrowed even further, perhaps the latter 'editing help' one into checking for run-ons, comma needs, and informality. Even those three steps could be narrowed, right? And the major stages are not simply linear, either, not for the better writers, the flexible ones who might re-plan after writing, for instance. In short, achieving this outcome necessitates objectivity, the ability to see the big picture, even when the image is yourself.

What would the old man say to him right now, at this moment, if he awoke and saw him standing there? "Go away," most likely, maybe followed by his favorite: "*You* made your bed?" The old man would dress him up in his failures, wrap him up tight, make sure that the blame was all on a son who'd been given *everything* and earned *nothing*.

Now look at him! Not so sure of himself, not so in charge! In *bed*, no less! Oh, he'd taken the right steps to be here now, alone with the 'patient,' prepared to take the big step, the one that would actually change things. Not everything took the swing of a sledgehammer. Some *swings* were subtle, calculated. He'd watched the front-desk security guy and noted his process, like clockwork, every two hours, day and night. The poor sonofabitch probably couldn't wait to get up and walk around the grounds, probably did some loitering out there, too, maybe had a cigarette or something more pungent, but no longer than nine minutes. He had clocked all the guards, *all Spanish guys*, eight to nine minutes, plenty of time, more than enough, for they all took their time, noticed no threats.

Night came earlier now in October, so it was dark and quiet when the guard slipped out into the early evening and began his leisurely stroll to circle the long three-pronged building. He was ready. Nobody in the alcove, behind the security desk, or even in the Ward C corridor. No noises but beeps and occasional snores and moans, but not many of those either at this way station. Peaceful and silent, just as it should be on the step away from oblivion. Soon! The doors were all open, these 'people' were going nowhere.

Just five doors down, the old man lay in perpetual sleep. With just a little tug (the plastic gloves were not an impediment), the plug slid out, and the machine's lights disappeared. Good! No nurse would come running in to get a flat line hopping again. He stood up, looked down, gazed on that familiar face one last time.

"Daddy want a cracker?" he whispered, taking a plastic bag from his pocket and removing a blob of grey and white, saltines smashed and mixed with tap water, *no DNA anywhere, coppers!* Apparently, the old fellow *did* want crackers because his mouth hung open, big enough to drop a golf ball in, and that's what he did, just dropped the cracker gob in and then used his finger to push it down some. *There!* He looked once more into the plugged hole, from which no noise leaked out.

Then he put an opened cracker packet on the side table near the bed (he had wiped it down with rubbing alcohol), peeked out the door, and hurried away, feeling elated, wanting to sing. "Bing, bang, boom!" thought the Cracker Man.

The security guard was still on his grounds check, the empty station vulnerable but still somehow a little threatening, an air of authority in the space behind the desk. *Frightening for some, maybe*. The intruder stepped into the off-limits space and bent down to stare at the video recorder, right where he'd peeked in and seen it on previous scouting missions, definitely not 'visits.' The buttons showed images, not words, but the left-arrow one was obvious: Rewind. He pushed it, heard the little clunking pause, a metallic gulp, and then the rushing whirl of the rewinding tape. Time eating itself. The guard would return, hear that sound, and immediately stop the tape and click the start button, whichever that was, maybe the one with the star. Or maybe the tape would rewind completely and then just start again. Either way, the intruder's entrance would be taped over, the evidence erased. An old man had woken from a coma, mindlessly grabbed a cracker or two mindlessly left on the sleeper's table, choked for a bit, and died. Just another accident, one that might even be covered up, or maybe the nursing home could even be sued! Oh, what a thought that was! *Whatever*, it was just another forgettable exit from a building crammed full of forgotten lives and repetitive deaths. Maybe this one would be just a bit less common due to the moist mass of crackers in the dead man's mouth and the unplugged monitor, a tinge more mysterious, something for the workers to whisper about on their endless rounds, but after the bagging and tagging, the pace would go on. *Gurneys in, gurneys out*. Almost like breathing, the pulse of this place and all the homes where the near dead went to become chiseled names and final numbers, the flotsam of the past.

Flotsam? That was almost poetic. Good ol' Diggerson would have loved that!

The mysterious death at Breezy Seas was investigated and did make the local news, mainly because of the unplugged machinery and the crackers, both of which confounded everyone. Ana Cepatos was interrogated twice, saying, "No-oh-o!" over and over again when grilled about the crackers. Nurse Addie, other nurses, other aides, doctors, front-desk personnel, even the sparse Ward C visitors, all were interviewed, and none revealed any leads at all. Even the front-door video had malfunctioned, rewinding and taping over the previous twelve hours. The old man's death was ruled 'suspicious,' boxed, and forgotten. The funeral was attended by a couple dozen mourners, one of them a grown child, who stood above the coffin as it was lowered and who all day long vowed to anyone who'd listen that Breezy Seas would pay for its negligence.

"Your face looks like my ass!" Digger was remembering telling Anna his new joke earlier that evening and seeing the look on her face, which was no doubt funnier than the joke itself, even though he'd set it up better than before, with a little pre-story about nature's 'being cruel.' That seriousness had juxtaposed well with the twist, at least that's what Digger had thought, yet Anna had coughed more than cackled. He would have to try the pun on someone else, maybe Lou, and for some reason he thought of George North, too. George had once told him that very few of the professors ever said 'Jack squat' to him, let alone stopped for a chat, that Digger was about the only one. A friend to janitors and adjuncts. Yes, Digger would tell the joke to George.

It was currently late at night or early in the morning, whichever description best fit 2 a.m. Definitely 'late at night.' It was his and Snodo's second backyard foray in just a few hours, the first of which had been interesting due to Digger's next-door neighbor, Graham, who'd been digging in his own yard. Digging in the dark of night. "Hey, Graham!" Digger had called over the fence. "You searching for gold back there?"

Just silence, no more shovel sounds. Just the wind. "Graham?"

"Yeah, Digger, it's me. I'm just burying something."

Digger giggled, partly in relief that the silence had in fact turned into his neighbor.

"Not Donna, I hope," Digger had laughed. He thought of her because he hadn't seen 'the wife' in weeks.

Graham made the sputtering sound that people do when they try to laugh but can't quite muster it up. "No, no. Don't tell Donna, though, but I'm burying a rat, just a rat."

A pet rat? His neighbors had no pets that Digger knew of, not even a goldfish. "A pet rat?" Digger had called out over the fence, immediately thinking of Anna's song "Round and Round," by the rock group Ratt.

"A pet! Oh, God, no. Are rats pets now? No, I found this one in the driveway, dead, don't know of what. I didn't know this neighborhood had any rats."

Digger had said that 'all neighborhoods' no doubt had rats, and his neighbor had responded, "Maybe so, maybe so, but don't tell Donna. She'd freak out! She'd probably want to move."

Digger felt worse for the rat than for his neighbor's wife, and since Snodo had been ready to go back in, the two men had traded goodnights. But just as Digger was about to open his door, Graham had called out again, "Matt, don't tell Donna about the rat!"

Three hours later, Digger was again out back with Snodo, and he giggled about his earlier encounter with Graham. Unless Donna were deaf, she must already *know about the rat.* He looked up at his neighbor's house and then past it at the dead-of-night sky, which was glittering with stars, not a cloud to be seen. Snodo was nosing around a bit more than usual, hadn't squatted to pee yet, so Digger kept his eye on her so that he could prop up the leash and keep her from falling into her own urine. Then he decided to keep the line taut and to gaze up again instead. The stars were very bright and twinkly, and the "What a Wonderful World" line about the 'dark, sacred night' drifted through his thoughts, soon replaced by the fictional Mr. Flood and his lonely trek through the night. Digger wished that Mr. Flood and all those real souls like him could have stopped drinking and instead been nurtured by the rich beauty of the universe, not immobilized by its vast empty spaces. Emptiness, darkness. How different was Mr. Flood than Paul Smith, or Eliot Gladstone, or even Tobias Mann, even Diana Pell? *Even me?* Digger stood beneath the canopy of stars and pictured predators and prey, imagined the rush of adrenaline that each brain supplied when needed, and decided that serial killers had some justification in nature itself, in the call of the wild. He wondered at the odds of crossing paths, let alone working down the hall from, two serial killers and realized that the statistics would be astronomical, beyond reason, absolutely fictional, more insane than his own protagonist's adventures, Billy D Wilder. As high a number as stars above.

With Anna nestled in their bed, Digger no longer felt the sadness of such celestial scenes, but rather its richness, despite the old dog at his feet. He liked the cool October air, the whisper of winter. Perhaps the cold settings were one reason why he was attracted to Nordic mystery writers, such as Henning Mankell. He'd just read a story by a newly discovered Swedish writer, Karin Fossum, called *The Indian Bride*, and had been staggered by its beauty and sadness. Digger could certainly remember such sadness, for decades ago he'd pushed it down into his black river, where for so long it had whispered his name at times, such as when he woke at night and looked around the bed to find Anna. He had lived with the sadness, and it was still there. For him and for all people, it flowed along with Time. Maybe it was Time.

"Nighttime thoughts," reflected Digger, and then Snodo peed at last. He held her up, he would always hold her up. For as long as she held on, he would, too, for sacrifice was a part of love. The sliver that made the feeling real, meaningful, true.

As he turned Snodo toward the house, to his bed with Anna, Digger detected a movement to his right, up in the second floor window of his neighbor's house. Graham, *keeping watch for killers and Nazis*. Or just making sure that the rat had stayed in its place. Digger pretended not to notice the surveillance and led his dog inside, lifting her up three of the four steps. Snodo had lost weight, yet seemed lumpier.

The next morning, after Anna had gone to school and before his own start to the workday, Digger called his mother. After three rings, she answered, slightly harried sounding as usual, as though he'd caught her in the middle of something, and immediately asked about Anna, then about Snodo, and then about him. Then she asked what many people still did: "Do you remember anything about 'that time'?" She did not mention the most recent criminal activity for one simple reason: Jean Diggerson's son had not informed his mother about the vandalized tombstones, had not even told her that he and Anna already had a stone, having anticipated a response along the lines of "That's ridiculous, Matthew!" Maybe it was, but Anna's symbolic gesture had made Digger happy. Someday soon, he would have to take a picture of their stone on the hilltop and explain it all to his mother, just not yet. For one thing, with no cell phone, Digger no longer took any photographs; for another, some things a son just did not tell his mother.

The Diggersons' gravestone was back to normal, though, as he and Anna had seen for themselves a few days past. Digger thought he could see a hairline crack across the back, but when Anna couldn't, he decided that he was seeing what he expected to see. A typical human reaction. They'd brought sandwiches, chips, and Cokes for a cemetery picnic, laying out a blanket before their stone, and Digger said that someday they'd be lying pretty much as they were then, "just six feet lower." Anna had laughed and said, "But I thought you wanted to be cremated." Snodo had wandered around a bit and then stretched out in the sun, her back legs splayed like a frog. Dogs and sun. Even on a scorching July afternoon, a dog would lie in the sun for a bit. Even when he and Anna had opened their sandwiches, Snodo had not gotten up to ask for a share.

His mother was worried about her cat, Rachel, who apparently was acting odd, not eating all her food. When

Digger asked whether that wasn't normal for cats, in other words being picky, Jean Diggerson had said, "It's not normal for Rachel." His mother could be a bit prickly. For the past few years, she hadn't mentioned her age, the actual number, quite so much, perhaps not wanting to jinx her chances at reaching the next decade—the 90's—but with that milestone now crossed, his mother punctuated the entire conversation with dead stops at '90.'

"If it would ease your mind, Mom, why not take Rachel to the vet's?"

"I'm 90 years old, Matthew. I drive only when necessary. You'll see that when you reach my age. If you do! You always seem to have colleagues who want to do you in. Did they ever find that Gladstone fellow, the one who drowned?"

No, they never had. As with Danny Jones, the troubled student whom Digger had tried to save two decades past but who'd thrown himself from the Bay Bridge and thus disappeared forever, the sea had accepted Eliot's body and decided to keep it. Digger pictured bones gleaming in the deep. What was his mother saying now? The son's mind had drifted to work, to teaching later that day.

Jean Diggerson hadn't noticed her son's distraction. "When my own mother passed away, you know I was quite young, Matthew, so when she passed and then my father not long after, well, it's not easy to no longer be a *daughter*, to not have that *role* in life anymore. You lose part of yourself. Who are you? You will find out someday, Matthew, and that day's not too far from now, when you're no longer a *son*. You don't know it, you're too young, but you will. When my mother passed away, as I sat with her, she said, 'Is this it?' and then, 'This is it, Jean, this is the end.' She could not believe it. That is how it will be, you will see."

The words 'nature's cruelty' came to Digger's mind, and for just a second he thought about telling his mother the worm joke. Instead, he summed up his agreement to her soliloquy: "Life seems long, until it isn't, right?" Soon after that, they concluded their phone conversation.

At OVC later that morning, Lou Knightly stepped into Digger's office before class and said, "I dreamed last night, just like your Billy D Wilder character, all his flying dreams and desert dreams, and doesn't he have a drowning one?"

"I think so," said Digger, "but sometimes I forget what I write."

"Check this out," said the tall man. Older now, Lou's face looked bigger, more skin, his lip licking even more prominent and a bit obscene even, as though tongue appearances were reserved just for young men, like skate boarding. "You can use this dream in your next book, for Billy D. I'm on a lake, in a row boat or some little boat anyway, and I'm accompanied by a white rabbit. Yeah, Angela and I have no pets, I never had a pet rabbit, but there it is, jet white, big ears. You have a white dog, right? Well, suddenly the rabbit falls in the water, or I think it does; it's in the water anyway, and I'm trying to get to it. I'm rowing or using my arms to pull up alongside the rabbit, but it keeps drifting too far away, you know how dreams are? Frustrating. So I end up in the water, and I grab the waterlogged white rabbit, and I toss it back into the boat, and then I'm in the boat again."

"Pretty exciting dream so far, Lou," laughed Digger.

"Well, then comes the nightmare. I look down into the water and see this big, dark shape go by, you know, like a shark, a big shark. But I was in a lake."

"What would it mean, Lou, your dream? To use it for Billy D, it has to relate to something, like a clue or a suspect."

"You're the mystery writer, Digger, but couldn't it be something dangerous coming, just gliding by, or something beneath the surface. The monster, the villain. Maybe a warning. Ask Lana about it."

Digger giggled because Lana wasn't real: she was his protagonist's one real regret, the love that he let get away. "You mean 'Anna.' Lana's a character in my books, one who never even appears."

"Fiction merging with reality, isn't that what you say? Write what actually happened. How are the books selling, by the way? Raking in the dough?" After the questions, Lou's tongue tip did its thing, slurping across the upper lip.

Digger shook his head and explained his failures at using social media to promote his books. He was negligent, added just sporadic Facebook posts, didn't use Twitter, or Snackbox, "or whatever it's called, Lou. I could make little videos, somebody suggested that to me. I could probably do all sorts of things besides my lame Facebook begging posts."

"At least you have something to post," said Lou, and Digger had to agree with that. "How do your parents like your books? Or your mother, right, didn't your father pass away long ago?"

"He did, a car accident, back before I was here at OVC. But my mother loves my books. After the first one came out, she cradled it in her arms and said, 'I love this book!' When I think of my poor sales, I remember that image." Then he remembered that the tall, thin, lip-licking man had said something recently about his mother's having passed. "I'm sorry about your mother," he added.

Lou licked his lips again, Digger's imagining a 'slurp.' His colleague seemed a bit lost in thought. "My father died, too," he finally said. "He joined my mother. I don't have any parents. That's an odd feeling."

"I'm sorry about your father, Lou. Ironically, my mother was saying the exact thing to me earlier today. She said that it was hard not to be a daughter—or a son—anymore, hard to lose that role in life. Just this morning, she mentioned that about an hour ago."

But all that Lou Knightly said was that "it wasn't so hard." Then the tongue came out, made its pass. The lip licking made Lou look hungry, distracting the other man. After Lou left, Digger remembered that his colleague was fairly newly married, and although he'd meant to ask about this great change in life, those long Knightly legs had carried the Chair far away by now. Lou hadn't mentioned his beloved. He was no longer a 'son.' Surprising that Gloria hadn't initiated an email *alert* about Lou's fallen father. But Digger then turned his attention to his 11:00 class, the immediate responsibility.

Through his first two classes, he thought of Lou, of sons, of his mother, and even of his silly worm joke, and before he knew it, Digger had returned to his solitary office. Anna would be back home by now, by noon, in fact. She would take Snodo out and perhaps do a little painting. Digger wanted to hear her voice, but as the phone rang for a third time, he thought that he might be disturbing her and was just about to hang up when she answered, a little out of breath, making him think of his mother again.

"Nature can be cruel," he said, and Anna laughed.

"Oh, I know all about cruelty and worms," she said, adding "I was just out with Snodo. She's so old, Matt. It's sad."

"She's still happy, though, still has that life spark. We'll know when it's time. That's what Sarah Palmer, the vet, said about Simba, that I knew when it was time and called her in. We'll do that with Snodo, too. Maybe it will help me to remember the time with Simba. Sarah's told me about it so often that I almost can see it myself."

"Repetition becoming reality," said Anna, and then "How's classes?"

Digger said that they were going well, "remarkably free of problems. And yours?"

"No un-coachables. Not yet, anyway."

Digger laughed, hearing his own made-up word. "You know what I say, Anna, right? You can have one or two un-coachables, just as long as they don't sit near each other and breed!"

"We definitely don't want our students *breeding* in class, Matt! And about nature's cruelty, don't go hanging out with your worm friends on the way home today."

After hanging up, Digger thought about worms and friends. His worm friends? *What friends?* Then he remembered Graham's rat. Anna might like hearing about his nighttime encounter, but she'd feel bad about the rat. Digger wondered why it had died in the first place. Had somebody else, another neighbor, set out poison?

A few hours later, two more classes and one more office hour completed, Digger left his empty office, passed by the hallway's closed doors, and thought about what to surprise Anna with for dinner on the way home. Friday late afternoons at OVC were almost monastic: a near total absence of human beings! Most teachers seemed to prefer a morning schedule, even Anna did, and Digger wondered if he liked afternoons partly for that reason: not to avoid Anna, but to surround himself with more empty spaces, more peace. Then Digger spotted a human. He smiled.

George North was cleaning the History Department's hallway, down at the far end, so Digger called out to him. "George, heh, I've got a joke for you!" George stayed where he was, rooted by his mop perhaps, so Digger walked down the hallway that mirrored his own. All the history professors' doors were closed, too, apparently empty.

"First," said Digger as he reached the other man, "you need to make a comment about nature, saying something about its violent side, its 'cruelty.'"

"Nature can be cruel," said George North without smiling, but then he did, perhaps in anticipation.

Digger giggled in expectation, too. That was exactly the opening he needed for his joke. "Oh, I know," he began. "I've seen nature's cruelty many times. In fact, just recently I came across two worms. They were out on the sidewalk in front of the Administration Building, you know, trying to cross the concrete after a hard rain. They were having a tough time, wiggling about the way they do. One was a little pink on one end, and maybe that's where the *cruelty* originated. The other worm, seeing the pink one wriggling about, said, 'Hey, your face looks like my ass!' How's that for *cruelty*?"

The other man said nothing at first, but slowly his modest smile widened (like Diana Pell's!) on the old young face, and then George North slapped his thigh and bellowed, "Your face looks like my ass!" Then he laughed and laughed, so loud that Digger himself stopped. "Oh, Professor, I'm going to steal that joke. Did you think it up yourself? Of course, you did, you're a writer. You must come up with all sorts of jokes, eh?"

"Not often," said Digger, "but I'm glad that you liked that one. You responded better than my wife did, but I added some details this time."

"The proof is in the details, eh? That sounds like something you might have told me in writing class, you or that old blowhard Professor Mann. Whatever happened to him? Oh, that's right, one of you teachers stuck him with a knife; now I remember."

Digger let George ask and answer his own questions and then escaped the odd janitor by thanking him for enjoying his joke so much and hoping that he'd have a nice weekend. George said odd things, but nobody had ever responded so warmly to one of Digger's jokes. That was the loudest noise he'd ever heard George make, and the laughter had been real.

"Oh, they're all nice now," said George North before Digger disappeared down the stairs, and then the remaining man turned away and resumed mopping. *Just like he was as a student,* thought Digger on the steps, descending. He *tells* but doesn't *show.* Retreating, Digger realized that he'd never seen George do any other cleaning but mopping, and then he thought of that image. Could any scene be lonelier than a solitary man mopping an empty hallway?

CHAPTER FOUR

THE TERMINOLOGY OUTCOME

Any educational course carries terms and concepts specific to that field of study, and writing is no different. Students need to learn the definitions for content-oriented terms (e.g., free-writing, revising, paraphrasing, topic sentences, valid evidence, etc.), grammatical issues (e.g., run-ons, dangling modifiers, wordiness, colons, etc.), rhetorical concepts (e.g., ethos, pathos, logos, false analogy, post hoc fallacies, etc.), and even a teacher's specific acronyms. If students fail to understand a certain term, how can they analyze their own writing for that topic?

This was bliss, this scene, all cozy on the couch with Anna, ensconced in the triangle of soft light from the television, sipping white wine, listening to the late fall winds gathering strength and purpose, with a big black cat purring on the floor, experiencing his own dream scene of peace. Only Snodo was missing, and Simba, of course, but the lion dog's ghost still clung to the white one's shadow. Snodo's personality had once been big enough for more than one dog.

"Where's Snodo?" said Digger, but Anna didn't know, concluding that she was "sleeping somewhere, the poor girl."

Digger looked around the room for a puddle of white. Outside the living room window, the air looked blue. "It's twilight time," Digger said. "My mother would call this the saddest time of day, but I love it."

"Me, too," said Anna, "but I know what Jean means about the sadness, the end of another day, night coming, darkness. My mother didn't like 'dusk' either."

"Maybe for mothers the twilight reminds them that their kids have grown up and don't need them, that they're gone. The end."

"I would think that 'that end' would be pretty peaceful."

"You're preaching to the choir, Anna," Digger laughed and then shifted the topic. "You paint nice twilight scenes."

"I like to have it peeking through a window. The slanting light and shadows are fun to work with, the tones."

"Speaking of tone, where *is* that little tone setter?"

Digger got up and found Snodo in the kitchen, flopped over beneath the table, not a usual spot. When he scooped her up, the white dog opened her eyes, and Digger sank into their depths. "Hi, Snodo!" he said into her face, and she responded by closing her big brown eyes slowly, peacefully. Whereas she'd once been a thirty-pound bundle of muscle, Snodo now felt light and somewhat fragmented, like a ten-pound bag of baked potatoes. Drooping her over his left arm, Digger stroked her head and then placed Snodo in the corner of the couch, where she'd have a little space but still be close by.

"She's so old," said Digger, and the two people looked at their dog, fast asleep again. "You should paint her, Anna."

"I was just thinking the same thing, just that image, Snodo asleep on the couch."

"Kind of like *Master Bedroom*, Andrew Wyeth."

Anna plucked her cell phone off the coffee table, clicked some button, aimed, and completed her photo of Snodo. She showed it to Digger, who was impressed by the clarity. I still don't ever want a cell phone," he said.

Anna laughed. "You know, some change is good, Matthew Diggerson!"

"Some," said Digger, holding a thumb and forefinger about half an inch apart.

On Friday nights at eight p.m., they usually watched *The Joy of Painting* on PBS because they loved Bob Ross, his sweetness and positivity. Anna said that serious artists would look down on Ross' work, but that she loved him, too. She told Digger about painting, about perspective lines, about wetting the canvas with a little spray bottle so that the paint would spread and blend, about letting the brush do the work instead of adding details with littler brushes. Anna said that she'd paint Snodo with acrylics, using both warm and cool colors, adding that acrylics dry quickly and that the paint blends the way the artist wants it to. "It's all about values," she concluded, "the contrast of light and dark, adjusting the values and designing the painting in thirds, which can be vertical. You start with dark and work toward light. You apply the acrylic paint pretty thickly, too, to have more time to blend the colors."

Digger was a little lost, yet he asked no questions, because he liked to hear Anna talk and knew that she liked to speak about painting, just as he did about writing. *Light and dark*, yin and yang. Digger knew all about the dual sides of life, even of people. He pictured Eliot Gladstone's head as it spun around the waters of the Whirlpool, the way his glasses had reflected that orange sunset light and then gone clear, round and round, his circular glasses flashing with fire. Now that would be a picture!

According to his neighbors, Graham and Donna, a couple needed to hold a good fight every so often, perhaps once a month, but Digger and Anna never fought and rarely even argued, the precursor to a battle for many. And he never wanted to be apart from her, even when he was writing and she was painting. Digger never took his wife's presence for granted, repeatedly celebrated it by bringing home fish and chips (as he'd done this very evening) and sometimes champagne (white wine on this night), and the couple would often sit out on the deck, even in cold weather, and watch Snodo's and Bumper's explorations and antics, listening to a distant neighbor's flagpole ding and sometimes too loud voices from their closest neighbor. For Digger, his and Anna's relationship was a light, a beacon in the dark of Time, a star still singing, not dead. Anna had said once that their relationship was getting better and better, but Digger had just smiled. He didn't see how it could get any better.

"My Dulce-Anna," he said and kissed Anna's forehead, resting right beneath his chin. Then he conjured Don Quixote's voice and sang the combined name twice.

"Does that mean I'm your princess or a prostitute? Wasn't Dulcinea a 'working girl'?"

Digger just smiled. He couldn't remember if Dulcinea had been a whore. Probably, since Quixote had seen what he wanted to see, a glass-half-full view. "This is my quest," the writing teacher sang softly, "to follow a star."

"No matter how hopeless," Anna cut in, "no matter how far."

Digger giggled. *Bliss*, he thought, and then he looked at Snodo, felt a little shadow. Values, darkness and light.

The next morning, Snodo walked away from her food bowl, but a few minutes later she ambled back and emptied it, albeit slowly, as a fist rose up through Digger's chest. Sorrow, and its accompanying chariot, a hard little rolling ball. Snodo, his white dragon, becoming grounded at last. He thought of how his mother would always ask whether Snodo had 'calmed down a bit' and how he'd almost expected this dog to defy Time and simply roar through the years. Roar like a lion, like his beautiful Simba. Nobody beat Time.

Digger opened the back door and watched Bumper stroll nonchalantly down the porch steps, and then he scooped Snodo up, carried her down to the lawn, and held her harness taut as she relieved herself. Maybe Snodo would like to romp around a bit. Digger went back inside to get coffee and then stared out the window at his two pets, at the morning layered over his little piece of back yard, his heaven. A handful of sparrows were zipping about, annoyed at the dog and especially the cat. How they used to love ferreting away with Simba's golden fur tufts. Snodo's hair was different, not double coated, so the little birds had no interest in those wispy, white strands. He sipped and watched the scene.

When Anna came into the kitchen, she said, "How's Snodo?" and she frowned, a V forming between her eyebrows, when Digger said that she ignored her food at first but then ate it. Anna felt sorrow, too, its slow rise. The two people watched the two mammals and all the annoyance of the birds, who didn't seem to know where to land or what to do.

Digger wanted to change the tone, elevate it, so he focused on the birds and said, "I think a good name for sparrows would be 'chirpsters.'"

It worked, or maybe Anna was just playing along. "Can you hear them? That's adorable, Matt! Chirpsters! It sounds like what cavemen would have called all birds."

Digger hesitated and then said, "I think I resemble that remark," making Anna groan. She didn't care for that silly cliché. Digger added, "Chirpsters look a lot like Keystone cops, crashing all about, changing directions." When Anna expressed her lack of familiarity with that term, Digger said, "From those old silent movies, a dozen crazy cops riding in and pouring out of a car, chasing the hero from room to room, bonking into each other and leaping up, all the motion speeded up the way those old movies did it. You don't remember them?"

"Maybe," said Anna. "I'm picturing some heroine tied to railroad tracks, but why were they called 'Keystone cops'?"

"Who knows?"

"Google probably does."

"Nobody knows but Google," Digger said adding, "That should be a new cliché," and then he giggled softly. Outside, Snodo had flopped down near the gate, Bumper had returned to the back door, and the Chirpsters were now ignoring them both. The two people stared at the white dog lying in the grass and felt sorrow, like barometric pressure, begin its ascent.

It was a rare weekend without any papers to grade, and Digger felt a peaceful malaise. Although he continued to take occasional notes for a fifth Billy D Wilder mystery, he didn't yet feel the obsession that writing those books always created. Maybe he felt too happy to write, despite his old dog, or maybe down deep he was just too sad about Snodo, down in his black river, where all the anxieties and insecurities flowed from the past into the future. *Loss, loss, loss.* That's what the river whispered, quieter than the winds that never stopped along the seashore. When a human chose to live along such water, the wind became personified, a constant companion, sometimes even a wicked thing, grabbing and moaning, complaining, relentlessly probing to undo humanity's efforts. A henchman of Time.

In the afternoon, between college basketball games, Digger decided to do some Facebook promoting of his books, a responsibility that he tended to shirk. He called social media 'Ego Media' and Facebook posts 'Selfishies,' but Anna twisted his view a bit, saying that her art students constantly took selfies with their works and that she herself had taken advantage of social media by creating websites to showcase their work. Digger shook his head up and down a bit to acquiesce and thought of his own website, usually neglected. When he logged on to it, he found that someone had emailed him, three times in fact.

"Look!" he called to Anna. "I have a fan!"

"Probably some lonely housewife," said Anna. "I'd better have a look."

When he clicked on the first email, the message was a short one: 'Hack!'

"'Hack'?" said Digger.

"Maybe you shouldn't read the other two," said Anna, but Digger couldn't help himself. Both were short and similar.

"My number one *fan*, who thinks I'm a 'hack,'" said Digger.

"It sounds like something Professor Happy Rock would have said. When was it written?" Digger checked. Two years ago. *Not Eliot*, gone eight years past.

"Even if Eliot returned from the dead, I can't see him going on Facebook." Who would bother? Somebody used to online life, *a millennial*.

"Matt, why don't you try replying to the person? Maybe he'll slip up and let us know who it is."

"Anna, you're thinking about those gravestones, aren't you? You think this guy—or it could be a woman, you know, one with big biceps—you think that they're dangerous, don't you? Now don't start trying to convince me to plug in that motion detector again!"

But Anna didn't laugh at Digger's half joke, just stared at the screen, that forehead V getting bigger, nourished by thoughts, such as the 22-caliber bullet that still slept within his temple. She sometimes mentioned it.

Digger hit 'reply' and typed in this: "I'm sorry that you don't like my mysteries. Can I ask why?" Then he hit 'send.'

"There, how's that, Anna? Now we'll see who my latest antagonist is."

"For a nice guy," said Anna, "you sure have a lot of those."

Digger giggled. Anna's face was so close to his, so he leaned over and kissed her cheek. "I care about just my number one fan," he said, and when Anna said that that was 'nice," he responded, "I meant Snodo!" Laughing, the two looked about for the white unicorn and saw her curled up motionless in her little bed. "What's more beautiful than a sleeping dog?" said Digger, and Anna just nodded her ascent. That 'V' had appeared again. *Why worry about Facebook?* Digger no longer cared about the negative email since by replying to it he'd released defensiveness, just let it float away or more likely sink below. Snodo's old age was what really mattered, Time being the real enemy, as usual. Time never flinched. From the motionless dog, the two people turned back to the frozen computer screen as though a reply were imminent, but wherever Digger's email went, it seemed to have died there.

In her basket bed alongside the couch, Snodo slept with nary a twitch, hovering deeper than any dream world, perhaps kept aloft by the soft threads of concern sent periodically from those two sources still in reach, just barely.

The next weekend, Digger was barraged by essays, and on the Monday before the following one, which would encompass Thanksgiving Break, Snodo gave her loved ones the message no pet owner ever wants to see: food apathy. That morning, she let Digger know (Anna was at OVC) that she was ready *to go* by refusing to eat, just staring at her bowl as though she no longer knew what to do with food. Between his paired classes that day, Digger returned home and tried to get Snodo to eat, in vain, for the dog didn't even sniff at pieces of sliced turkey, formerly one of her favorite treats. She just slept in her little bed, curled up, waking only when Digger carried her outside to do as necessary. That Tuesday, Digger canceled his office hours and took her to see the vet, Doctor Sarah Palmer, who could find no reason but age for Snodo's lack of appetite.

"She's panting, Matt. Trying to get more oxygen through her body." Snodo lay flattened on the metal exam table, her now prominent spinal column forming ridges, jagged, making her look even more dragon like. Digger thought of Puff, the magic dragon. He 'lived by the sea,' too, just like Snodo, who had also always been a *frolicker*.

"But Snodo's not in any distress, right? I don't need to put her down now, here?"

"Just keep an eye on her, and when the time comes, you will probably want us to come to your cottage, right, same as for Simba?"

Exactly. The cottage, right where Digger himself wanted to depart life, in his harbor, surrounded by present and past love. "But you'll be closed for Thanksgiving, right? What about

Friday or Saturday, or Sunday even?" Suddenly, the short break seemed not like an ally, but an obstacle. Palmer wouldn't be available from Thursday through Sunday. The vet told Digger about an emergency service, but it was a fairly long drive and not the cottage either.

"We'll have to leave it up to Snodo," he said, and Sarah Palmer gave that reluctant smile that was really more of a frown.

The rest of that Tuesday, Digger and Anna stayed by the panting, lethargic Snodo, and Digger slept with the dog that night on the couch. In the morning, Snodo stayed asleep, even when Digger lifted her up and carried her outside an hour after he had arisen. He held her up by the harness as Snodo relieved herself. If he had not scooped her up again, she would have collapsed into her own pee. She completely refused her breakfast. An hour later, Digger called the vet's and made an appointment, just as he'd done a decade earlier but still could not remember. Snodo had no more time; she would suffer over the Thanksgiving break.

Noon. One o'clock. Two o'clock, three. Four o'clock, and at five Digger held Snodo and cooed at her, and then Anna joined them, a huddle of love. When the sound of crushed stone rippled outside the bedroom, Digger even jumped a bit. Anna wiped away a tear and went to the back door. Sarah Palmer appeared, along with an assistant, one of the front-desk women, the entire practice made up of females. "I'm sorry, Matt," said his long-time veterinarian. The assistant held the bag, saying nothing. Sarah introduced her as 'Lily' or maybe 'Leslie.' The humans all looked at each other, face to face to face. Nobody could think of anything to say.

Snodo just slept, even after Digger laid her on her blanket on the couch. "You said that we said goodbye to Simba outside, Sarah, but it's too cold today, and Snodo loves this couch. She's spent about half her life on it. I should have replaced it long ago, but I probably never will. I got shot on this couch." He giggled a bit at that unexpected statement, and Anna frowned at him. The other two woman were busy.

Snodo slept, even when the assistant attached the stent, even when the first shot entered her body and eased her even deeper. Snodo slept, even when Sarah said "Ready?" and when Digger mouthed 'yes' and Anna nodded her head, unable to speak. Anna was behind the couch, crouched down and stroking the white fur, pulling gently on Snodo's Mohawk, and Digger was on the front side, pushing his fingers up the slope between the little dog's eyes, over and over. Snodo slept, but just as the vet began to squeeze the killing solution into the tube, the white unicorn opened her brown, brown, beautiful brown eyes, lifted her head, looked directly into Digger's face, and then shifted her head, stared up at Anna, before drooping down onto her paws again and closing her lids.

Focused, Sarah Palmer had not noticed Snodo's goodbye, but her assistant had and said, "Oh, my God! She just thanked you, both of you!"

"Yes," said Digger with some effort. "Snodo said goodbye." But Anna said nothing. She had too much emotion in her throat, that ball of sorrow.

Within those pair of seconds, all the time it takes between life and death, between future and past, Snodo's life force vacated her small body, leaving four humans in a circle, each thinking slightly different thoughts, but all woven around a little white dog who was no longer there.

Prior to the vet's home visit, Digger had dug a hole close to Simba's grave, remembering what Sarah and his neighbor Graham had said about the one he'd shoveled out ten years back. Having forgotten that experience (with Eliot Gladstone's 'help'), Digger discovered again that the soil turned to sand fairly quickly and that he needed to build walls to get far enough into the earth, so he'd used the same crate lids that he'd employed once before, not realizing that fact. The hole took him an hour to create. When he finished, he thought of Graham's rat and of its living family members, so he dug some more, further into the sandy bottom. *Like digging water*, he thought. It was hard to create a hole, but Digger knew that it would be tougher to fill it in, not physically harder, but mentally.

After Sarah and her assistant left, both quiet, meek almost in the face of death, Digger and Anna sat around Snodo's body and petted her still. Bumper came into the living room and sat down between them. The cat's eyes blazed golden, and he purred, the sound actually audible in the peaceful scene. Bumper had almost never made a noise, so when he meowed once, loudly, both humans jumped in their skins and then laughed. They patted the Tom cat on its big black head and then settled back into their vigil, as dusk descended on them all.

Out back, Digger and Anna sat on their knees near the hole and still touched Snodo's white hair, so long and thick, so full of life. Digger was about to lower her down, but he waited, not sure for what. Looking at the deceased Snodo, Digger thought of the poet who wrote about a baby's passing, the speaker's looking down at the little body and wondering how it could "hold" such a giant presence as death. Snodo held that immensity now, silent and unmoving, the factualness of a future without the white pony's fire and joy, an end stop, a period the size of a boulder, a big black hole. Digger could not remember Simba's lifeless body. In his mind, the Lion Dog was always running, her long body see-sawing happily, her mouth stretched wide, grinning over the sheer immensity of being in the present. Immensity! Snodo's body looked so huge and yet so small. Yin and yang again, black and white, life's inescapable duality. Opposing twins.

Anna was crying softly, Bumper had left to explore the beach, and Digger was completely still, completely quiet, because this was one of those moments in life, one of those pivotal points that signaled a change, a shift in the road, a transition. After Digger lowered his dog into that black hole, existence just would not ever be the same, for memories would play a larger role in Digger's mind. Soon, the figures of the ghosts would outnumber those with still-beating hearts.

"You know," he said to Anna, surprised that he could even use his voice, "the older we get, the bigger the past gets. The more we carry the past in our minds. And I don't know if that's a good thing or bad. Probably good, necessary."

"It's like that lady from Lark Rise to Candleford, you know, Margaret. It's like what she said to Thomas, the postman, that loss is just a part of love, that that's the 'bargain' we make when we love, that we have to accept the loss." Anna sniffled.

The bargain, yes. Digger shook his head in agreement and lowered Snodo into her hole, dark and dry and oh so far away.

CHAPTER FIVE

THE AUDIENCE NEEDS OUTCOME

College writers tend to think of their 'readers' as just the professor, but this view can get them into trouble because they might think that this educated person needs fewer explanations, that the teacher will 'obviously' see the connections between point and evidence. Maybe the professor would note the links, but papers are graded on how well they transmit information, for the most part. Thus, all college writers must balance their papers' contents between being too obvious and too obtuse: what does the reader already know versus what does he or she need to learn?

With Snodo's passing, Digger discovered the truth in what his mother and his would-be killer, Eliot Gladstone, had once said about a second parent's death: that the second one took the first again and created a complete void. That's how the cottage now felt sans dogs, for Snodo had carried off Simba again or perhaps even for the first time since Matthew Diggerson still remembered nothing about his first dog's exit. He and Anna mentioned Snodo every day, remarking at the remarkable look she'd given them both, a last love connection. "Some people would say that we're just anthropomorphizing," Digger had said, "that we saw what we wanted to, but I know that Snodo was saying goodbye and 'I love you.'" Anna had agreed every time.

Time ground on, uncaring, unsentimental, and the fall semester approached its end, the final day of classes in December's second week. No snow had yet fallen, but the Diggerson's back yard looked less barren due to the addition of another dog statue, a perky Scottish terrier, the closest likeness that Digger could find to his white unicorn. He angled it a yard from the German shepherd that announced Simba's grave, again the nearest concrete dog to his lion, and the two memorials now gave the yard even more depth, both visually and spiritually.

When Digger awoke, he heard Anna in the kitchen, doing the dishes, probably, and when he sauntered into the kitchen, she said, "Quick, what song's in your head?"

Digger giggled. "You wouldn't believe it, he said, and you'd never guess. It's 'Billy, Don't Be a Hero.' Do you remember that old tune? I don't even know who the band is." Anna didn't even know the song, couldn't remember it, but she said she'd look it up on YouTube.

After she left for her final morning classes of the semester at OVC, Digger let the song play through his mind. *Billy, don't be a hero, don't be a fool with your life.* It was very catchy, but why on earth had he caught it? Had he heard it on the radio? The name 'Billy' made him think of Bill Jacobs, the long-time adjunct who leaned way right and who Digger had once assumed might be a murderer. He wondered if anyone had ever sung those lyrics in jest to Bill Jacobs. His wife, Gemma, maybe, but now she was gone. Then Digger imagined Bill's swinging a sledge hammer. No, neither image really fit, the first being too playful, the second too physical and angry— even for Bill. Then he thought about Anna, all thoughts inevitably attracted to her. What song had been in her head that morning? She hadn't said, and preoccupied with his own ditty, Digger hadn't asked. He thought about calling her, but instead he phoned his mother since he hadn't talked to her yet that week.

"Oh, Matthew," his mother said, adding, "This is an unexpected surprise," a statement that made Digger feel a bit defensive since he'd talked to her every week. *Mothers and guilt!* No matter how old the child became, too.

"I'm just calling to make sure that you bought me a Christmas present," Jean Diggerson's son joked. "We'll be coming on Christmas."

"Oh, I'll have something for you, and for Anna, maybe a couple of somethings. And how's little, oh, I almost asked about Snodo. I'm sorry, Matthew."

"That's fine, Mom. I don't want to forget Snodo or not talk about her, or Simba, too. It's like what you said about your own parents, though. When the second one goes, in this case, Snodo, then the first one finally leaves completely, too, and that's how I feel about Simba."

"You know, Matthew, I almost asked you about Simba, too. But I've been thinking differently about your father and sister, my own siblings, my parents. I think that the older we get, the closer our deceased loved ones become, not further, closer. Time brings them closer, Matthew."

Digger thought that Time did just the opposite, brought the loving closer to the dead, but he kept this to himself. Instead, he asked what they were having for Christmas dinner and whether he and Anna should bring something.

"Oh, whatever, Matthew, whatever you want to bring. I'm just not interested in food anymore, and I'm never really hungry. I'm ninety years old, you know, so I can't smell the food so much anymore or even hardly taste it."

"How about salmon?" Digger giggled because his mother tended to complain about the only dinner he ever cooked her on past visits.

"Oh, my God, Matthew! Oh, why not, why not salmon? Whatever you want, that's fine with me."

Digger asked about Rachel, his mother's last cat, ancient now (she was still "a little off"), and then about her brother, John (still "deaf as a doornail"), and then about Carol and Mary, her older sisters (still "oblivious"), and then about her neighbors, specifically Jan Green (still goes to church and "drops in whenever she wants"). Digger tended to let his mother's anxieties flow right past him, and he was actually glad that everything in his childhood world seemed to be the same. Change tended to be for the worse, he thought, an attitude that his ninety-year-old mother would definitely share.

"I'm looking forward to seeing you and Anna," his mother had concluded, and after hanging up, Digger looked out back at the two concrete dogs, especially the new one. Whoever had created that Scotty mold had certainly captured Snodo's verve for life, or 'piss and vinegar,' as his mother would have called it. With both its head and tail raised, that Scotty looked ready to bark, and Digger could easily hear Snodo's varied vocalizations, especially her scream of happiness when he came home and saw her through the back door. *Oh, memories!* So beautiful, yet each a little dagger, a little pain, a silver stiletto of light through shadow.

As he ate a cheese omelet, Digger thought about the song or non-song in Anna's head and contemplated calling her, but she'd still be in class. He'd ask her later, when he was home again himself, with half of December and most of January stretched out for both teachers, space in time just waiting— after the 'final exam' projects.

But what had Anna said before leaving, that she was going to do a little shopping that evening? Yes, and that she'd bring dinner home, that was it! That she probably wouldn't be back when he returned but that he should wait and not cook something. *Don't cook!* That was fine with him. They would celebrate the semester's end with take-out food and some wine. Digger checked the fridge. White wine, they had!

When he went out the back door to drive to school, Bumper usually left the cottage, too, and then he'd come back in when Anna came home. In his mind, the back yard had become 'Snodo's grave,' for Digger couldn't walk out on the porch without his eyes and mind turning to the spot beneath which his little love lay. *Two of them now.* Guarded by stone. The dog statues made him think of the toppled gravestones from Ocean View Cemetery, but it was just a passing picture. Then he wondered why Anna had said that she probably wouldn't be home when he came back. How long would she be shopping? Probably, she was coming home and then going out again to synchronize her shopping with dinner, with the take-out food. He wondered what she was getting him for Christmas. He had two gifts already for her, a new copy of Fossum's *The Indian Bride* and a somewhat expensive shoulder massage contraption, sort of a heating pad with some kind of kneading capabilities, since her shoulders continually seemed sore. And since Anna loved Midori, he would get her a big bottle of that green liqueur, too, and then something else, maybe some earrings because his wife couldn't get enough of those! Maybe a framed picture of Snodo, an old photo. He and Anna would open most of their gifts on Christmas Eve and save just a few for the trip to his mother's on Christmas day. What would he get his mother? *Useful things.*

As Digger was thinking about the holidays, Bumper slipped out and headed for the gate, without a backward glance. *Oh, well. Cats were cats.* Digger looked at the two dog statues and pictured the cool, dry graves beneath.

"How's tricks, Matt?"

Digger jumped slightly and then smiled. Graham's head was half over the fence that separated him from his neighbor's land, and Digger thought, *Good fences make good neighbors, but step ladders block good fences.* Graham was just a bit odd, but a 'good' neighbor nonetheless. Sometimes the unpredictable man called him 'Digger,' at others 'Matt,' even during the same conversation, and Digger wondered how Graham's mind could switch back and forth like that, informal to formal. At least he never called him 'Matthew,' a moniker left to just one earthly human: his mother—and perhaps to Anna when she was upset with him, those few times.

"Tricks are good, Graham, and you?"

"Can't complain, or I could, but what good would it do?"

Upon hearing that old cliché, Digger smiled again, and a soft giggle slipped out. "No good at all, my friend," he said, adding "Where's Donna?"

"Out, out, always out. I could complain about that, but no sane husband complains about his wife, eh? And where's your pretty little missus?"

Graham's answer had conjured up Macbeth, so Digger replied, "Out, out, too."

His neighbor missed the reference, but most people would. Digger was just trying to amuse himself a little, to rise above the dog statues' grey auras. When he asked his neighbor about 'any more rats,' the other man froze up and turned the question around, tangibly releasing concern when Digger said "no, no rats." Then Graham looked toward his house, his eyes narrowing, and his head disappeared.

"Gotta go, Digger," came from behind the fence. Then "Be good."

Do good, thought Digger; *be well*. Short conversations make good neighbors.

In his small Toyota, Digger scanned the back yard again before departing, taking in mainly the two stone dogs and one flesh-and-blood cat. Bumper had returned and was lying—what he and Anna called 'bread-boxing'—in the middle of the yard, facing the departing man. With golden eyes just half open—slatted, Bumper looked wilder than even the swooping seagulls. If Digger hadn't known and loved that black cat, the lidded-eye image might even have frightened him.

Hours later, alone in his office, Digger realized that the fall semester was basically over, just papers to grade now, and he had over a week to finish them. He was humming and softly singing, "Billy, don't be a hero, don't be a fool with your life," but after that he couldn't remember many words, something about "wife" in the next line. Earlier, he'd said 'Merry Christmas' to Gloria, Lou, Todd, and to that blinking adjunct, Jay, along with another new part-timer whose name he couldn't remember, *Ben Something*, and that failure had made him feel a prickle of guilt. He should try harder with people, take more of an interest in them. Then he heard someone making a racket in another office, and when he heard "Shit," he knew it was Jolie.

She seemed not to be in the holiday spirit. Digger decided to put his 'should' into immediate action.

When he peeked out his office door, noting as usual the lack of a Dream Board, the pale square spot on the wall, he saw Jolie trying to juggle a stack of papers, but when a few flopped to the ground, the woman swore again. When she looked up and saw a grinning Digger approaching, the frustrated professor said, somewhat sarcastically, "Digger, pardon me! Expletives so close to Christmas!"

"Let them fly, Jolie, but you wouldn't need so many if you just collected papers through our online course site. It's so much easier, honest, and you can't *drop them* on line."

"To each his own. I need to hold the paper and to write right on it, to connect with the student, and that's just how I'm going to do it, no matter what you say."

No preaching to the choir here. Oddly, the "Billy" song flashed past his thoughts, so he asked Jolie if she ever "ran into" Bill Jacobs "out in the real world." Jolie said "Who?" She had no idea whom Digger meant. When he started to explain that Bill was an adjunct, it occurred to him that he and Jolie had had a similar conversation once before, and Jolie must have felt the same because she ended his explanation by saying "An *adjunct*," stressing the "ad" as though asking a question. Digger, however, realized that with that single noun his peer was instead making a statement. Down the hall, Digger noticed the janitor, George North, perpetually mopping, and again he thought of 'Billy' and of 'Bill Jacobs.' Like Lou and Gloria, Bill would've talked to Digger about his books, probably about how bad they were! But he would've acknowledged them, unlike this cantankerous woman. Maybe getting to know people wasn't such a great idea.

Jolie was gathering up her papers, dropping others, and as Digger bent and helped her, in his mind he was alone again in this hallway of peers. *We're just ghosts to each other.* Tobias, Diana, and Eliot were still all as present here as everybody else, all just walking the halls and disappearing behind doors. Vampires into their coffins, ghosts into their tombs. The Grammar Nazi, Gwena Schmidt, had retired long ago, and then the full-timer Mary and the part-timer Bill. Digger missed them, those older peers. Now he had become one, old. Is that how Jolie pictured him? She'd finally corralled her essays, and Digger remembered her penchant for saying "Of course" in response to many statements. Of course, of course! It always bothered him, and he remembered telling Anna about it. She'd said that it was human nature and then told him about an interview she'd once seen with Michael Jackson and Oprah Winfrey. In answer to nearly every question, the infamous musician had said, "Of course," but that he'd used the words sweetly, drawing out the second one: 'Of cooooooooooourrrsssse.' Communicated like that, the answer was not dismissive, not as much, anyway. After that story, Digger had always tried to convert any 'of course' that he heard into Michael Jackson's. Yet he usually failed with Jolie's.

"I hope those essays are easier to grade than to hold," he smiled, waiting, waiting.

"Of course!" said Jolie, and Digger giggled, the first full-fledged release since Snodo's death.

Feeling reckless, thinking of the newly betrothed Lou Knightly, he asked about Mary, about whether or not she and Jolie planned to "tie the knot."

"The noose, you mean. Listen, Digger, it's not 'Gay Marriage' that I object to, more like 'marriage' in general.

Most married people would be much improved as individuals if 'split asunder,' don't you think? You'd agree if you'd known my parents."

Wanting to say, "Of course," all stretched out like Michael Jackson's, Digger focused not on Jolie's question, but on her wording, on 'split asunder,' on stones, and on the crack after 'Listen' on his and Anna's memorial. Jolie stared straight into his eyes, awaiting a response, challenging an opposing stance, and Digger noticed lines running down the outside of each dark eye, a pathway for tears. Jolie wasn't much younger than he.

"As a person joined, split, and joined again, I whole heartedly endorse marriage, Jolie. If it's the right person."

"Of course!" she concluded, adding, "You're just like my brother, Mr. Successful in his eyes, just nobody else's!" With that abrupt opinion, his long-time colleague turned and left, still wrestling with those papers. Digger resisted the urge to holler about online grading. Then as she disappeared, Jolie yelled to wish him a 'happy holiday' and 'good winter break,' nice thoughts, even if delivered while walking away, faced away.

After she left, Digger returned to his office, fulfilled the last half hour of time, stared at the reaching shadows of the library's clock towers, at the descending darkness, listened to the gulls, sang "Billy, Don't Be a Hero" louder than before, and then locked up.

George North stopped mopping, took off his headphones, and cradled them around his neck. Digger could hear heavy metal, a repetitive base guitar, and the 'song' drove "Billy" from his own mind. George was smiling, and Digger once again thought that this 'boy' looked far older than he could possibly be. What, thirty-five, thirty-six? George was missing a tooth on the bottom row, toward the back, but he didn't seem to care. His grin even widened.

"That's one angry lesbian!" the former student laughed, confusing Digger for just a moment, until Jolie and her falling papers came back to mind.

"We're all a little nuts when we have so many papers to grade," Digger said, but he laughed, too, his usual response to being shocked.

"Just give them all A's and enjoy your time off," smirked the janitor, but Digger didn't rise to this grading bait.

"What about you, George? I've forgotten if you're married."

"No way!" said George, reminding Digger of Jolie, in fact. "Never been roped."

"And your folks, are you going home for Christmas?" Digger thought of his mother.

No again, Professor. They're gone. If I joined them for Christmas, I'd have to spend the day in the cemetery. Too cold, and what gifts would I get but a frost-bitten ass?" Then George laughed at his own joke.

Digger smiled, mostly because the word 'ass' had made him think again of his own worm joke. "My wife and I love cemeteries," he said. "We even got our own tombstone already." Why did he tell *this* man *that* fact? Something to say.

North shook his head east and west. "Bad idea," he said. "You don't call the dead, Professor. You never call the dead."

"I'm sorry about your parents," Digger said. "They must have been young."

"Not so young," said George, and then he smiled. "Your age, about that. And they avoided a lot of pain, and neither saw it coming, you know, the end."

It. Death. Digger had 'seen it coming' twice, three times if the forgotten living-room scene with the bullet were recalled, once in his own kitchen and a dance with Paul Smith, the latest on a long plank out into the sea with Eliot Gladstone. Twice, he remembered having 'seen it coming,' but neither time had it *come.*

"Well," said Digger, "that's good about avoiding pain, and fear too. Do you have a dog or cat?"

"No," chuckled the janitor, as though that idea were ludicrous. "I'm here too often, and the administrators wouldn't want the janitor walking around with a dog, like you do sometimes."

Digger was being dragged down, the way he could be when his mother was particularly anxious, but then a little song started up: "George North, don't be a hero, don't be a fool with your life."

"You got any more jokes, Professor?"

George was referring to the worms, of coooooooorssse, and that made Digger laugh. He thought about singing his little George-North song. "No, that one was about my quota for the year."

"My ass looks like your face!" laughed the custodian, soon to be the building's last beating heart as the December night descended. "I wish I could have told that one to my father!"

When Digger pulled into the cottage, twilight had almost hooded the earth, and Bumper awaited him on the porch. Anna's white car wasn't there, but he hadn't expected it to be. He switched on the blue LED Christmas lights, which illuminated the two stone dogs, fed the cat, who kept up a steady purring throughout the meal, and then decided to wrap

Anna's gifts, the two he already had. Rummaging through a bin of old X-mas packaging, Digger found an ancient tag from his father to him. The tag, the size of a movie ticket, was golden and red, perfectly preserved in the crate, and it showed a smiling Santa Claus, full of life and good cheer, apparently having just ridden the chimney down, standing before a lit tree and holding a large bag of gifts. When Digger turned the old-fashioned picture over, he read, "To Matt, from Dad.' The little message startled him, traveling through time to remind him of something elusive. He looked at the card again, both sides, and imagined a Christmas past when he'd first read the card, that small magical moment in Time. *Something for me.* There was a beauty in that little piece of paper, a reminder. A gift for me, something I'm about to open, long ago. What was it? What was the gift? Could it have been anything as beautiful as this simple tag? Digger smiled and put the old gift tag on top of some wrapping paper he planned to use. He would show Anna his father's message through Time, love's conquering of death.

By six o'clock, Matthew Diggerson began to wonder when Anna would return, and by seven, he speculated on why she hadn't called. By eight, he called her cell and got only a voicemail that her box was full, and by eight-thirty, he considered going out to search for her. By nine, he just paced and paced. At ten, the front doorbell rang.

She knew exactly where she was going. To get *chocolates*. Matt loved the chocolate covered jellies, she loved the raspberry creams, and that little candy store off of Ocean View's main street, Maple Avenue, had the best of both. And just down the street was the sporting store where she'd pick up his sneakers, white Converse high-tops, just like he always talked about wearing as a kid, before that brand became such a fad. Matt always joked that *he* had started the canvas Converse mania. He would *flip* over those sneakers, and she'd checked his ratty old pair to find the right size. She'd thought that the nostalgic sneakers would help lessen the sadness of Snodo's passing, and the jellies wouldn't hurt, that's for sure.

In Bradford's Chocolates, she was surprised to be the only customer, but the man behind the counter said that they'd been busy that day and would get busier at night the closer Christmas came. "When people need another gift and rush out and panic," the man had laughed, an older gentleman, probably the owner, working late. Although she knew already what she wanted, she perused the display cases and complimented the variety of choices. He made them all himself. Then Anna asked for the combination box of jellies and raspberries. He gave her one raspberry chocolate for free, and she was still enjoying it as she exited the shop. Reveling in the side-street's yuletide atmosphere, which needed only some softly falling snow, Anna decided to walk. It was just a little cold, and the sports store was only a couple blocks up, only about six cone lights, she saw, each streetlight creating a little stage, a circle of civilization holding back the night. The street was also lined with trees, many of which had been decorated with string lights. She and Matt would have to drive through here and admire the ambiance. Too bad they couldn't walk these sidewalks with Snodo.

It was so peaceful and empty. The lights seemed to shine just for her. Cradled in her left arm, the box of chocolates felt like a dictionary, and Anna Diggerson smiled at the image of opening them and partaking on Christmas Eve night, or maybe they'd bring this gift to Jean's and share in the rich bounty.

Christmas Eve, she thought, and then she heard a motor revving, approaching fast. Focusing on Matt and chocolates, Anna Diggerson didn't recognize danger, not in this fantasy scene of lights and soft darkness.

In the following instant, she felt a sudden blow and then nothing, her last thought being a car crashing through Christmas Eve and a box of raspberry creams.

The bell sounded loud and foreign as it bounced around the living room, and Digger jumped from the couch at its call, moving toward the door like a vampire's victim, helpless against the summons, numb. Since nobody ever used that door but an occasional UPS man with a package, it creaked like an old coffin and revealed an even more ghastly sight: a man in uniform, a policeman. "Is she okay?" Digger said immediately and then, "Where's Anna, my wife?"

The emotionless man stood completely still and said, "Anna Diggerson has been in an accident, a hit-and-run off of Maple Avenue, and she's been taken to Ocean View Hospital, to the ICU."

Digger turned, ran for his sneakers and coat, and charged out the front door past the policeman. "Thank you!" he said in passing and then simply forgot about him. When he backed out of the driveway, he barely registered the cruiser parked in the street, and Digger just zoomed away. If anyone had asked him about that drive to the hospital that dark night, Matthew Diggerson wouldn't have been able to add even one detail. He was suddenly parking and running to the ER door, asking about 'Anna Diggerson,' and hurrying down an impossibly long hallway, where he found another nurse and then a post-operative room. As he stood over the bed and the nurse described the situation (stable but critical, a coma), Digger saw that they'd bandaged the left side of Anna's head with wrapping, but Digger pictured the damage, a concave symbol of despair. *Blood, a broken skull.* What did that wrapping hide? *No*, Anna wasn't broken, for she looked so peaceful, so beautiful, all draped in white, marble carved by a great Italian master. *The Angel.*

I've killed an angel, Digger thought, his eyes moist and losing focus. She escaped me and my magnet to death, but I drew her back and then Time caught her as it does everyone around me, a lure for loss, for murder and for accidents. For the Great Sweeper, Time. If she hadn't returned to save him, Anna wouldn't be in this hospital bed, her head wrapped in bandages.

Digger suddenly realized that the nurse was still there, still talking. The doctor was waiting for the swelling to subside, but they'd *stopped the bleeding.* Anna's brain was dealing with the trauma by shutting down, and Digger thought of his own coma, how his brain had done the same. The staff would *re-evaluate* Anna's condition in the morning. She'd received a *serious blow* to her head and upper body. "Drunk drivers!" the nurse concluded, but that idea didn't register in Digger's mind until later, after the nurse had left. Only individual words floated up, like with that shaker-ball toy he had as a child, the softball-sized black ball. Ask the Eight Ball? He and his sister, Emma, would ask questions, shake the ball, and then learn the answers. Emma had grown tired of the toy before he had, but she was older. What questions could he ask now? *Drunk drivers* floated up, unbidden, and Digger thought of a question. How could a car have struck his wife so high up? And then another, that Maple Ave was full of trees, so how could a drunk driver had avoided those? This was no accident, Digger concluded, no *drunk driver*. This was *war*. This was Paul Smith again! Eliot Gladstone again! But who this time, and who really cared, anyway? What really mattered but this beautiful woman lying comatose and being a finger flick from death? From *Snodo*. Digger thought of Snodo and could easily picture the white dog curled up and sleeping on this white hospital blanket. Then he thought of Bumper, alone in the house, and that was fine. Bumper would be *fine*.

Digger laid his head on Anna's hip, and seated, bent over, he slid down toward unconsciousness and then slipped into his black river, into rapids and rocks. His vision narrowed until he saw nothing at all, perhaps just a distant tunnel of light, the despair rolling over him and sweeping him down, where the black river grew colder and emptier, until nothing remained at all, just darkness, and he clung to it, cradled it, called it to take him away. How much could one man lose? Whole lives had slipped away, been snatched away, great invisible pieces of living, *gone,* and what was left? Neighbors who knew his name, colleagues who said hello in passing, students who changed every four months, memories. His mother loved him, but who else? Simba was gone, and now Snodo, too. His father, his sister, and Anna? Had he lost Anna twice? Gone again but this time for good. How much love could a person lose? Was it measurable, like blood? Each love lost, a pint of blood, and when the soul had suffered one more lost love, then that was it. Too pale, too thin, bloodless, dead. Too many pints! That's how Digger felt, seated but dead, a stone statue, and he liked it almost, the bitterness, the righteousness, the release. Time had won, as he knew it would, as it always did.

He knew, too, that no despair could ever go deeper than this, that a person could lie damaged and dying and not feel this heart-crushing horror, that a gradual death like that would be rimmed in a soft peacefulness, but not this despair, a thudding jolt that would throttle any sensation of tranquility and leave just its sprawling languid corpse. And he knew then that any future life would always be like this, coldly moistened in despair, that going on would mean plugging that great dark wall of water with a thumb that could never be extracted and comforted, never treated, without the sick alienation trickling and then flowing and then bursting out. *No joy in Mudville*, he thought but couldn't remember why that phrase would bubble up, perhaps an attempt at lightness, a shared moment with Anna, but gone now, gone with everything, just flat carbonation, no flavor and almost no substance.

No more chirpsters, thought Matthew Diggerson before disappearing below the surface of his black river, where consciousness could not go.

When he awoke, Digger discovered that he'd slumped back into the chair, that his back ached, and that Anna looked the same—completely still and oh *so beautiful*. She looked pale and eternal, and Digger remembered her telling him the same thing when their roles had been reversed. With one big difference, though, for he had awoken. Would Anna? *Of course*, he thought, and then he said it to himself again, said it as Jolie would: Of course! And he'd be right here when her blue/green eyes opened. His eyes were dry, and he remembered a talk they'd had once about Digger's lack of tears, how his continual losses had not opened up those ducts. Digger had said that 'only literature' could make him cry, and Anna had recounted a trip they'd taken to a regional theater to see a community production of *Death of a Salesman*, how Digger had suddenly started 'blubbering' when Willy Loman told his boys about his own brother's walking from the wilderness a self-made man, and that Biff and Happy had to 'hit 'em low and hit 'em hard' at football. Digger had said, "I don't know, something just welled up in me. The passion of Willy, the futility, the emptiness of talking to a ghost, his trying to find meaning, it's all just so beautiful, Anna. That's really the reason I lose it. So beautiful and so sad." She replied that Digger had repeated that performance when they saw Richard Kiley in *Man of La Mancha*, and that's when Digger had first said, "My Dulce-Anna."

Later that morning, the nurses gave Digger Anna's cell phone and told him to go home and rest, that they'd call the cell if any changes occurred. Digger thought of Bumper. Had he let him out last night? If not, what must Bumper be thinking, alone in the cottage? Perhaps Digger had suffered another memory loss because after the image of the cop at his front door, he could remember almost nothing, just Anna stretched out pale and motionless in this bed. *Don't let that be my final Anna image!* he thought and thought, and after he drove home, he again realized that he'd been in some zone, that he could barely remember driving.

Bumper was looking out the back door, quite at ease, and he stepped out and off into the yard when Digger opened the door. Maybe the black cat was a little put out since he ignored Digger's whispered greeting, those few useless words. Digger knew that he must either whisper or roar, and he feared losing control and smashing things. The nurse had said something about a drunk driver, an accident, but what about all those toppled gravestones last summer? Why just *their* stone and all those connected to the past two murderers? From the Tobias Mann days, Digger pictured the little cop, Doyle, and his disbelief in coincidence, and the ball in his gut ignited, started to flame. If the cops weren't going to investigate this 'accident,' then he would. He'd find that driver and smash him six feet into the ground.

Matthew Diggerson could feel the violence of the earth's spinning, the splash and swish of his rising black river, and he focused both into a line of vision out the window, out into the bay, where the winds were whipping the water white despite just a few clouds passing in the sky. Birds were zipping about, chickadees and sparrows, having little disagreements, and his blue spruce was waving for a time out. Suddenly, he had the image of two little cats, black and white both, seated like bowling pins and staring up at him as he looked out the door. *Shyla and Skittles.* A lifetime ago and only yesterday, both at the same time. *One of Time's myriad tricks*, thought Digger. To make you think that the years were passing and then to strike, to rip something away. Snodo, Simba, Shyla and Skittles. Parents, siblings, friends. Anna. Anna!

The back yard suddenly darkened due to one of those clouds, and with the shadows the winds picked up, churning the waters even more and making his blue spruce go quite mad. *How 'cruel' nature could be*, Digger thought, and that word reminded him of something, a small light igniting, only to be swallowed by shadow. Then the sun returned, as did Bumper, and Digger found something to eat (out of routine, not because he felt hungry), sat at the kitchen table with a notebook, and started to plan. Although he knew that his students' papers would be adding up in his online course sites, he had other steps to take first, other responsibilities.

First up, Maple Avenue, the scene of the so-called 'accident.' Digger found the exact spot because a ten-foot rectangle of police tape appeared around a lamppost and tree—a maple, of course. Digger parked just past the tape and then discovered a chalk outline within the taped area. He pictured TV shows and dead bodies. Did a cop actually draw an outline around Anna as she lay there? *Impossible,* the paramedics had gotten there first, had taken her right to the hospital. This chalk outline was more of a circle anyway, sort of an X-marks-the-spot, probably just to give the cops time to think before they decided to shelve the whole incident under the title 'Accident.' Digger looked into the middle of the chalk outline, the blob, but the sidewalk within was no different than the one without. Anna's consciousness was not captured inside the circle. She wasn't in there, in that hole. Her consciousness had gone wailing with her and the ambulance to the hospital, and now it rested behind closed eyes.

The chalk oval ignited that ball within Digger's gut, but then he gathered himself, his logos, and looked around. Where had Anna gone? Who could have seen her? He would have to go from shop to shop, so he walked straight into the first one, a small restaurant. Although the hostess/waitress had heard about the 'accident,' they served only breakfast and lunch, so they were long closed when it had happened. The woman said how sorry she was and suggested the 'candy shop' next door. He stayed open fairly late, she thought.

A bell rang when Digger entered the candy store, which smelled sweet and clean, but Matthew Diggerson's senses were mainly off. Just sight and sound on, both pointing forward, like a dog's. The man behind the counter was older, both hair and a short beard slightly frosted, and he seemed to be doing paperwork. "Can I help you?" he said.

"Yes," said Digger, but he wasn't quite sure how to proceed. Then he just did. "My name is Matt Diggerson, and my wife, Anna, was in an accident outside last night. She was hit by a car. You can see the spot just up the street a bit."

"I remember," said the man, frowning. "Your wife had just bought chocolates—jellies and raspberries. She was just in my shop."

Digger's heart seemed to have stopped, sight dimmed and sound came up out of a hole. He thought that he should sit down, but only the floor was available. "She was here, Anna? How do you know?"

"Blond, attractive, a very nice woman," said the man, "and the accident occurred right after she left. I went out and waited with her. I called the ambulance. How is she doing?"

"She's doing okay," said Digger. "She's alive, unconscious right now, but alive, and thank you for calling the ambulance, for staying with her. Did you see the car?" Digger held his breath, waiting for an answer.

"Not really," said the man. "Maybe just a flash of blue. In fact, that's why I peeked out the door. Cars don't speed by on this street, and I even heard the motor revving. I wanted to see where the idiot was going."

So the car had been revving its engine, not slowing down, and Digger had seen no skid marks in the street, no attempt at avoiding Anna or even the curb. "Did you hear anything else? Did the driver swerve or stop, afterwards?"

The candy man came around the counter as though retracing his steps. He passed Digger, opened the door, and then looked back. The man was trying to put himself into the past. "I didn't hear or see anything after that flash of blue, that revving sound. Just your wife, lying on the sidewalk." He'd also noticed his box of chocolates, all smashed and spread out, but he didn't say this to Digger. It didn't matter.

"The driver," said Digger, "he must have hit the curb and popped the car up. My wife was hit in the upper body, and her head, too. She has a bad concussion." Digger didn't want to think about Anna's head beneath those bandages, the left side of her head, exactly where he still had a little bullet in his own.

"I saw," said the man, frowning. "I saw the blood, and I thought just what you just said, that the curb had caused the car to jump up. It wasn't an SUV or a truck that I saw. It was a blue car, not a big one, either."

"Did the police talk to you? Did they say anything about a drunk driver?"

"I did talk to a patrolman. I told him just what I told you. He didn't say anything about a drunk driver. The cops just ask questions, they don't answer them."

Digger shook his head in affirmation, for he'd had the same experiences with the police, for the most part. He thought of Doyle, who'd been a little different. Then he thought of the female cop, Zorn? What was her first name? She'd behaved pretty much as this candy man described. Digger thanked the man and wrote his name and number on a piece of paper, asking the concerned and helpful fellow to call him if he remembered anything else, feeling like a TV cop as he did so but not caring about that.

When he left the shop, Digger stood outside for a minute, looking left and right, thinking of the blue flash revving up and roaring by, flying. Then he heard the candy shop door open and the man calling him. "Mr. Diggerson, here. Take this; it's what your wife bought. It's for you; it was for you." He handed Digger a white box about the size of a couple bricks. It was heavy, too, a lot of chocolates.

"Thank you," said Digger, and he felt his eyes moisten. "Thank you," he said again, but then his voice constricted. He couldn't say another word. He just held the box, Anna's gift, and stood silently under the sun. The man returned to his shop, the entrance bell dinging even for him.

After a minute, the cold seeped in and Digger looked around him, found his car, but also saw a man shuffling away in the distance, a couple blocks away. He looked familiar, and suddenly Digger landed on the image of Bill Jacobs, bent forward, steering a clear path through unseen obstacles. Bill Jacobs? And in that moment the composition teacher wondered again if his old peer were the villain, *finally this time*. Not of Tobias' or Pinsky's or Diana's, or of those two women stuck in the darkness of some severed synapses, but of Anna's. After all, Bill lost Gemma, his wife. The distant man was still stumbling away; it would take him some time to disappear, but how fit did a man need to be to run someone over? Of course, smashing tombstones was another matter entirely, and that thought prompted Matthew Diggerson to get moving himself.

Next stop, Ocean View Police Department, and he'd been to the one-story building before, long ago it seemed, but then just yesterday as he pulled into a space in the back parking lot. He always seemed to get the same parking space, and Digger thought of his students, who usually chose the same seat, class after class. As he walked toward the door, the writing teacher told himself to stay calm, not to get angry in a police station, because he expected that they were doing nothing to find the driver who'd tried to kill Anna. That's what he thought, accident be damned!

At the front desk, Digger explained who he was and what he wanted, to talk to the person in charge of the hit-and-run accident from the prior evening. "Detective Busher," said the front-desk man, but he was "not available at this time."

The cop's neutrality rankled Digger, but he didn't show it, not yet. "When will he—is it a 'he'?—be available?"

The cop looked down, perhaps checking a schedule, and then said, "Sixteen hundred hours." Four p.m. Digger nodded, started to turn, but then turned back.

"Could I call him then? Could I have his number?"

The cop didn't answer, but he wrote something on a card, then handed it to Digger. A business card with the OVPD number and Busher's extension written in. Digger thanked the man and left. He might be at the hospital later, but he could use Anna's cell to call Busher.

Outside the police station, the maples reached skeletal fingers into the sky. Digger had seen these trees grow, the one near his car being twice the size it was when he'd had those talks with the short detective, Doyle, two decades back. Ironically, life seemed simpler back then, but wasn't that always the case? Wasn't that just one of Time's tricks?

CHAPTER SIX:

THE AUDIENCE INTEREST OUTCOME

Writers quite simply must know their audience, not only what information readers need (such as background facts), but how best to deliver it in order to maintain the writer/reader connection. When will readers want to see quoted proof? How best should a series of statistics be shown? What should begin the paper? How should it end? Should the main point be laid out clearly or led to more subtly? Should a comparison be delivered as a metaphor or perhaps just with parallelism? The correct answers require a consideration of audience. Writers create to be read.

Diggerson must be in Hell, *was* in Hell, for he'd seen it in the man's face. Haggard, expressionless. How did the man really feel inside? Alone, hopeless, futureless. Yes, all understandable feelings, and misery loves company, as his mother often said. When he'd veered his junky car at Diggerson's wife, hit the curb, and gone airborne, that had been a moment of intense shock and fear, but then joy, all at once, *amazing!* Amazing, too, that he'd not slammed into a tree or a post, that he'd landed, bounced, regained control, and sped away, whooping. Had he even hit the woman, though? A glance in the mirror showed her down, laid out, so he'd done something anyway, had created a nice path for the cops. *Into the weeds!* That's what the restaurant workers always said, the waitresses, when they were really busy and needed help, his help, although at all other times they never even noticed him. Diggerson's wife, somebody's *sister*. If he hadn't trailed her from the little house on Cottage View, he wouldn't even have known her, but he liked to drive by that house, thought that it looked like a nice place to live. A place where a man could breathe clean air, just a little salty, and actually see stars, not light pollution. A place where a man could watch TV without hearing the blather from other people's sets. Diggerson was way too lucky. Past tense.

Yet he was, too, he was *lucky*. He still felt like whooping, for nobody suspected him, not *this* time. The cops had looked suspicious last time, analyzing his reactions, looking for crackers, probably. This time, he was free since no cameras had caught him, apparently, or the cops would've come banging on his door again. Always cameras, cameras everywhere, even on people's phones. How was a person supposed to break the law these days! But in those rich places along Maple Avenue the store owners cared about only themselves, their own doorways, so they put up cameras just for themselves, their little spaces. He'd understood this immediately, even as he saw the woman leave her car to go into the candy store. Diggerson would've lauded his analysis and all his planning, avoiding the main road with the cameras on the stoplights, but much fell to dumb luck, too. Or just 'luck.' His father would've said 'dumb,' but he wasn't saying anything now. Who'd said that a person couldn't escape his past? Some damn fool! Time *did* eat the past. *You just need to help it chew,* he thought happily.

Even his piece of crap car had come through with hardly a dent, just one broken headlight, easy enough to replace, worth the $39.95. The right-front tire hadn't even blown, and maybe it was only his imagination that it now needed air more often.

Probably just some residual anxiety. That would be a good name for a heavy metal band: Residual Anxiety. "Round and round," he whisper sang as he worked, "your love will find a way, just give it time." *Ratt*, one of the greats, but he didn't hear them much anymore. The radio was *going to the dogs!* Everything was *pop* these days, little girls singing about all their sadness, as if they knew misery, and little white boys pretending to be black. Country and western, too, and how did that maudlin *shlock* become so popular? All those big-hatted idiots crooning about their lost love and whiskey needs. Round and round? More like round and stop, stop at pop. He wondered why Ratt had drifted into his mind, but he welcomed the old rockers, smiling as he sang, as he toiled away.

A month after Anna's 'accident,' she was moved from the hospital to Breezy Seas, and Matthew Diggerson saw life going in its usual circles, round and round. Once again, he was listening to Nurse Addie ("You must be patient"), hearing Ana Cepatos' musical exclamations ("O-oh-o!"), and waiting, waiting, waiting within a room down the Ward C corridor. Doctor Sam was no longer working there, and Digger missed the man and his funny accent, but not too much. Digger simply had little emotion for anyone but Anna, lying white and still in her bed, resting comatose between the living and the dead. Nurse Addie had said that her *vitals were good*, repeating that fact every day, and it helped the writing professor a lot, gave him hope throughout those long mornings and endless afternoons beside her prone form. As he read mysteries (old friends) or worked on his laptop (building his spring courses helped him to focus and fill the time), Ana Cepatos would come in and do her own work, smiling in greeting and in parting, saying nothing, though. What was there to say?

The cops certainly said almost nothing. By phone, Digger had talked to Detective Busher twice, both times ending with irritation at the man, who didn't appear to take the situation seriously and who seemed inept at both listening and speaking. Digger asked about the blue car described by the Candy Man, whose name Digger couldn't remember (had he ever known it?). Specifically, the composition instructor wanted to know if the police had canvassed collision centers and garages to find any blue cars with front-end damage. That question had been followed by silence and then by the usual, "We're doing all that we can." When Digger asked about drunk-driving reports from that night and about DUI's involving blue cars, the same silence and the statement dribbled into his ear from the phone, which Digger contemplated smashing against the wall—both Anna's cell after one talk and his own landline after the other.

Luckily, he didn't, because he used that home phone more during the latter half of December and the first weeks of January than he had in the prior two decades. Mainly, he talked with his mother, who always began with "How's Anna?" Sometimes Jean Diggerson would ask about Snodo before correcting herself in disgust, and then she'd say that Rachel was soldiering on, not quite normally. Then she'd tell him about her batty older sisters and stone-deaf brother, Digger's aunts and uncle, whom he never talked to on the phone. With this family information, his mother was trying to restore some normalcy in the present, but she couldn't help mentioning 'Anna' between most of her statements, saying most often that she'd be 'fine,' that he'd see, that she'd come out of this mess just as strong as before it. After these mother calls, Digger would smile and vow to tell Anna how Jean asked about her first, rather than about any animal. "That's quite an honor," he'd tell his sleeping wife. "My mother puts you before the cats and dogs." At least twice a week, mother and son had the same basic twenty-minute conversation.

Besides the uncommunicative cop and his opposite, Jean Diggerson, Digger talked to a handful of worried colleagues, none of whom had ever called him at home, not that he could remember, anyway, except for Gwena Schmidt, the long-since-retired Grammar Nazi, who listened almost as well as his own mother. Digger told his old friend about what the cops called an 'accident' and about the gravestone vandalism from last August, linking the two events by mentioning the smashed stones, especially Tobias' and the old janitor's, Pinsky. Gwena said that Richard's stone was in that cemetery but that it had been untouched, that she visited her husband every week. Digger asked if her name were on the stone, too, and she said that it was, that adding it now saved time later. Digger told her about Anna's surprise and their own stone at the top of the hill. "I suppose it was silly having a stone so soon," he had added, and then, "I hope so, anyway."

"Anna had been telling you that she's here to stay," Gwena had told him, "and she's still here, Digger, and will remain so. Don't you lose hope!"

He'd felt a little guilty getting this message from a woman who'd lost her own mate, her own love, but Gwena's motherly words did help him. Small connections meant something. They added up. After the call, Digger had realized that the Schmidt's un-vandalized gravestone narrowed the suspect pool to people from Tobias onward, but then he concluded that that epiphany helped him hardly at all. Whom did it lop off? Basically, just

Gwena herself, and she'd never been a suspect during any of OVC's colorful history.

Other colleagues had been, one of whom was Lou Knightly, the current Humanities Chair. He'd called Digger twice, expressing both remorse and optimism, back and forth, each time asking if Digger wanted to take the spring semester off or have a reduced class load (*No*, he needed the work). Both times, too, Lou asked how Anna was doing, but so did all the other full-timers in their single calls: Jolie, who sounded softer than normal; Todd, whose "sorry" was stretched out in the Midwestern drawl that still colored some of his words; Don Domberg, whom Digger knew from his days in Tutorial Services and who'd drifted apart from him in the intervening decades; Catherine, who sounded a little stiff even on the phone. Always quite 'upright,' Catherine was approaching retirement without swiveling her head left or right, turning into Diana Pell without the smile, without the poetry. Digger also heard from the introverted bachelor, Jeff, quiet and serious, who taught during the mornings and almost always left before Digger returned from his first classes. Although the two men had been colleagues for decades, Digger could go for literally years without seeing Jeff if not for meetings, such as the summer gathering of writing faculty. Once, when the two shared a committee responsibility, Digger had witnessed Jeff lose control—almost. Someone had said something slightly off color—had it been William Watkins?—and Jeff's face had bloomed pink to crimson in seconds, almost like watching a chameleon's color shift. But even on that occasion, Jeff had hesitated, shifting pigment, before parceling out his words as though reluctant to set them free. From Gloria, Digger had heard that his careful colleague could get quite angry in class and glower at students, but he didn't enjoy gossip, had never believed second-hand evidence, chose not to. Every story had multiple angles, some flattering, others less so, and that truth applied to all humans, not just to reserved ones like Jeff, who'd ended his talk by urging Digger to "ask if he needed anything, at any time." That call, out of all the full-timers', had almost broken Digger's reserve, and he'd had to force the "thank you" from deep in his throat.

Even a few part-timers phoned him, such as the cat-loving Patricia Pauley and Jay Moore, the blinking adjunct. Digger was especially surprised by Jay's call since he hardly knew the man, and afterwards he wondered about the one-time realtor. From selling houses to pedaling pedagogy, not the usual life path. Even a retired adjunct called to express his sorrow and well-wishes—John George, who'd already taken his leave from a secondary education job and taught composition classes ever since. After their talk—most of the words given by John— Digger wondered what the stately fellow was doing to fill his days. Lifting up grandchildren? Swinging a golf club? Reading, of course, but life required more variety than lounging in fictional worlds. Perhaps stone smashing and running over angels? *Silly thoughts.* Digger was turning everyone into a villain, as though they all harbored an incurable virus and were edging toward him with dripping noses. Ugh! The power of *pessimism!* He should focus on the fact that his peers had bothered to call, to take the time, but his talks with John and Jay had been short.

As was the returned call from Anna's mother, Deena Grimes. Digger hadn't called her right away, not until right before Christmas, and when he finally phoned her, he was relieved to get just her answering machine. He left a message explaining what had happened (what *had* happened?) and where Anna was, but Deena hadn't called him back, not for over a week, during which time Digger wondered if she were getting back at him for his taking so long to call. That sounded just like Anna's childish mother. Deena apparently hadn't even known about her daughter's lying in a hospital bed, unconscious to the world, making Digger feel a little guilty, which was probably the woman's intent. Later, Digger told himself that he'd been preoccupied and then busy with papers, but he knew beneath the surface that he just didn't want to talk to Deena Grimes, to the only person in the world whom he actually hated, whom he couldn't forgive for treating his precious wife so poorly for so long. But at least Deena hadn't killed Anna, as perhaps he had. Digger hadn't confided his theories to Anna's mother.

During one mid-January morning, a thin layer of snow covering the outside world, Digger stood at his back door and watched the ever-present sparrows feeding in his yard. The sparrows were just 'birds' now. No more 'chirpsters.' Everything was just what it was, no auras, just empty air, no notes, just sounds. Everything was a B-flat chord, and Digger thought for a moment about that note. B chords were hard to play on his guitar (bar chords in general), so he tended to avoid them. Since he'd sung no songs for weeks, he couldn't remember exactly what a B-flat sounded like, but it was no doubt a sad, 'flat' declaration, a note void of any emotion, the final 'e' on a falling *sigh*. Anna would *die*, he knew that now, knew it because the world emitted only B-flat notes, void of chirpsters, of Simba and Snodo, of fathers and sisters and little black and white feral cats, and soon void too of Anna. Digger closed his eyes and sighed, a long nasal exhale, a B-flat falling from a cliff, and that image almost stopped his descent because imagery added richness to life.

When the phone rang, Digger thought immediately of Anna, but if the nurses or doctors from Breezy Seas called, they would probably use Anna's cell phone, which Digger had somewhat forgotten how to use. He'd learned how to charge it up every night and kept it in his pocket at all other times, but he wasn't sure what buttons to push, if any. The landline rang again, and when he said hello, somewhat listlessly, his mother didn't even bother to return a greeting, just said, "Matthew, how's Anna?" He replied that she was the same and that he'd be going to Breezy Seas soon. He didn't want to call it a 'nursing home,' but that's what it was. His mother was silent, rare.

"We had this thing," Digger confided because he wanted to let some sorrow out, reduce the pressure, and because the silence gave him a chance. "Sort of a game," he continued. "Every morning, we'd ask each other what song was in our head, you know, what tune we heard after we woke up. We almost always had one, and sometimes the songs would be old, usually they would, for I don't know any of the new ones, all the pop stuff, and, Mom, I never asked her that morning. She was gone early, and I just don't know what song was in her head."

His mother just said his name, "Matthew!" Said it twice. Then she said, "Your whole life together is a song, Matthew, so don't fixate on that one morning. Don't be like me, always worrying about things that'll never even happen. Just be with Anna, and tell her what song you're thinking of now."

"No song, I have no songs in my head anymore." He thought about B-flat notes, which would be grey, maybe blue-grey, and that made him think of the blue car seen by the Candy Man. Could it have been blue-grey? Many cars were blue-grey, sort of a slate color. Why had he taken 'blue' for an answer? He'd always told his students to 'be specific' when they wrote, yet he hadn't followed his own advice.

"You will, Matthew. Both of you will. Just be with her and sing to her, and Anna will hear you. I'm ninety years old, Matthew, so I know about these things."

After the call, Digger decided to find out about the 'blue' and to take his mother's advice. He *would* sing to Anna, even bring his old acoustic guitar to Breezy Seas and strum out a few tunes, maybe Warren Zevon's "Keep Me in Your Heart for a While" or that older one, "Let It Be Me." Maybe Springsteen's "I'll Wait for You." Although he himself remembered nothing after his coma, not even his waking life the year before, maybe Anna would. If anything could penetrate unconsciousness, it would be music. Notes instead of words. The idea gave him hope.

Love and loss, he thought, looking out the back window at the cold beauty, the starkness of icy water and sky, the distance. Life's two great themes, one the goal, the other the obstacle. Then he added 'loyalty,' the glue, and went to the closet to get his guitar.

Before leaving the cottage, he looked up "Confectioners" in the Yellow Pages, wondering if he were the last American to still check those, and then he called the Candy Man. He said his name and then mentioned the accident to "my wife," which appeared to jog the man's memory. The man asked about Anna, and Digger gave his usual response, that she was still unconscious. He didn't like to use the word 'coma.' Then Digger asked the shop owner about the 'blue' of the car.

"Was it a dark blue, a light blue, a grey-blue?"

"I just remember a flash of blue," said the Candy Man, adding, "It wasn't dark, or light, or greyish. Just blue. Maybe not a robin's egg blue, but blue blue, you know?"

Digger didn't really know, but he sort of did. "It was dark," Digger said, "So are you sure it was a somewhat bright blue?"

"A streetlight's directly opposite my door, and all I remember is the engine noise and then a flash of blue. But it wasn't a dark or light blue, and for me to think 'blue,' it had to be pretty bright. But it was quick, you know, just a flash."

Digger thanked the man again, said that his chocolates were the best in the world, and apologized for taking up his time. The man hoped to see Digger and his wife soon. A nice thought.

On his way to Breezy Seas, guitar in back, Digger drove slowly by garages, looking for a somewhat bright blue car with any Anna-dents, the image fueling a fire that burned a bit brighter each day that the police failed to contact him. No doubt because they were investigating nothing. The *killer* might have waited to get his *damn car* fixed, holding off until 'things quieted down,' as fictional villains always announced to their accomplices. Still, during December, Digger had scoured every Ocean View garage and collision center, searching for blue cars with broken headlights, but he'd found nothing. And what would he have done anyway? The searches had been driven by emotion, but finally the writing teacher was turning to another part of his brain, to logic. A *blue blue* car, not robin's egg blue, but blue. The field had been narrowed again.

He'd parked his car out on the main road and walked, despite the cold. After the autumn situation with the dead man, the nursing home had probably added more cameras and other safety procedures, so he decided to reduce the risks. He sat on a bench along the long driveway and watched his breaths balloon and disintegrate, over and over. The cold January air bothered him just a bit, but he was warmed by the wrapped dough-like ball in his pocket and the opened snack packet. *The Cracker Killer!* If he succeeded, *when* he did, the papers would see the pattern and find a label to sell their rags. He'd dressed darkly and somewhat tattered because that was his plan: to wait for the guard's exit and then to pretend to scrounge around outside the door—for cans, of course, so he had a plastic bag with a couple in there already—and then to slip inside and plant a cracker ball in the woman's mouth. *Bye-bye, Diggerson's wife.*

On the bench, his breaths exploding, he heard his father's disgust over "a job half done! *Half done* means not done!" *Don't you worry, Daddy dear.* He would 'cracker' her, then Diggerson himself, later on, creating more paths for the cops. No need to rush these things, and he needed to erase one more face first, anyway, one more after the comatose woman, another divergence but a very pleasant one. Next month maybe. *We can always get what we want,* he thought, *because if we desire something enough, if it really matters, then we take the steps to achieve that outcome. What we want. Those that don't get it have simply changed their goal, or they never had one. It was all about goals, this life.*

Philosophizing made him feel good, strong, and he exhaled bigger and bigger ice bubbles, which sank and crumbled nonetheless. He didn't let his mother's ghost come hovering in, pushed thoughts of her and what she would think away.

Instead, he thought about his *junky* car, needed a new one, but not yet. The old one could still come in handy, and a new one now would mean owing somebody, being in another human's debt, even if it were just a nameless bank. No, if a person were erasing his past, then he couldn't be connected to it by *debt*. A new car would have to wait, maybe even until his parent's estate went through the system. If it ever did. *Damn irritating!* He felt the cracker ball in his pocket and heard the two cans clink in the plastic bag, reminding him of the present. Where was the damn guard? *Yo, Jose!* The cold began to seep into his layered costume, so he pulled the hood down further and stared at the big front door, imploring it to slide open. And it finally did, disgorging the guard, another skinny Spanish guy or maybe the same one.

When the thin man disappeared around the corner, he sprang from the bench and ran quite un-homeless like toward the front door, slowing down only to play his role. Then he stood before the doors, which slid open left and right, and ambled in, head down. The door to Ward C, always open on past visits, was closed, and when he grabbed the handle, he realized that it was locked. What's more, someone was in the hallway, and he realized with a sort of thrilling fear that it was *Diggerson*, carrying a guitar but looking back into a room, apparently his wife's, and saying something. Change of plans! Zig when the opposition zags.

Matthew Diggerson was saying good night to Anna, but something caught his attention down the hall, a shadow, a moving shadow. *Probably just the guard.* Anna looked so sweet and young, as always but even more so, and he stood in the door and stared at her. A few times, the staff had closed their eyes to the rules and let him sleep in the chair all night, but those next days had been hard, groggy. He needed his wits, to plan not only the next semester's classes but also his own investigation into the attempt on Anna's life, for that's what it had been, regardless of the authorities' conclusion. Earlier that evening, he'd called Detective Busher yet again and asked about Paul Smith, learning that Tobias' killer (and Pinsky's, of course) had been moved to a less secure facility due to good behavior and old age. "But plenty secure enough," Busher had declared. *Okay*, maybe, and then Digger had asked about Eliot Gladstone, about the lack of a body, for none had ever washed up anywhere. Busher had stamped Eliot 'deceased' and 'still in the ocean, just bones.' *How could he know, for sure?* They'd looked for activity on Gladstone's credit cards, for any sightings. They'd done this long ago, and Eliot Gladstone was gone. *But what about his brother?* What about him? Digger wanted to know what kind of car he drove, *what color*, but Busher had just grumbled and soon ended the call.

Saying "Goodnight, Anna," Digger turned from her and walked down the Ward C hallway, noting the silence. Hardly any hearts beating strong, none loud, and he thought of pond life now, the world covered in ice, just enough heart pulses to stave off the endless night. That's what Ward C reminded him of, and he urged Anna to keep beating. In the vestibule, he found no guard. *Must be out doing his rounds*, so Digger left Breezy Seas alone and made his way to the little lot where he tended to park, even though it seemed to be mainly for staff. He was used to parking there and fell into that habit, just like students who usually selected the same desks each class. *Habit*, he thought, and as he walked through the dark, he thought of killers and habits, looking up, listening for a speeding car and then for a shadow from the woods, for Eliot Gladstone and his club. Modus operandi, that's what TV villains all followed, MO's.

Out on the main road, a car whooshed past, definitely exceeding the speed limit, but it had been black, not bright blue. Digger was tired, but not hungry. He didn't seem to care much about food these days, and that fact made him think of his mother, who always dismissed any mention of lunch or dinner, saying that she didn't care, that food no longer interested her after eight decades. Almost a *century* old, Digger thought, fixating on that number: 100 years, a century. A *decade* versus a century. When he heard the latter, Digger always had to compare that word with the former, a memory device, the linkage highlighting the difference. In his mind, everything seemed to be a decade ago, but a century! That was an almost unimaginable number, yet his own mother was crawling toward it.

And he'd just left a hallway where the inhabitants' races were nearly run, past even the crawling stage. Each life leaking away in a little silent room. Not Anna's, though. *Not Anna's!*

With such thoughts bouncing from lightness to dark and back again, Digger reached his car, just two others in the lot, neither one blue. On the drive home, he imagined that he was being followed, that cars behind him carried enemies, tail-gating killers, and he hoped that they did! He wanted to do something, anything. But nobody followed him down Cottage Road or lurked outside his back door. Even his neighbors were asleep, apparently, and the lawns each held its dead. Dogs and rats. Only Bumper awaited him on the back porch, sitting up in that feline stance, feet all together, like a bowling pin. When Digger said his name, Bumper began to purr, a rumbling melody that rode the night's silence and turned the world from threatening to sweet.

In the kitchen, Digger fed the black Tom cat, checked the fridge for his own food options, and then cracked open a Bud Light instead. He stood in the kitchen, looking out at the shadowed back yard, the lights glittering on distant shores, and his head felt big. He felt big, enlarged, just a big head. He couldn't feel his toes or his knees or even his hands. Just his thoughts, floating near the ceiling. The room shrunk, and at the same time, the outside world expanded, the sky and clouds and dark blue waters, all grew impossibly big and threatening, huge beyond imagination, and suddenly Digger never wanted to go out there again, never wanted to leave this room. He stood like that and felt like that for minutes that seemed like hours.

Then something small made its presence known to his big head, something way, way down, and he was able to move a bit, able to swivel his big head away from the immense sky. *Bumper.* Bumper was down their looking up at him with those little golden galaxies of eyes, blinking slowly. "A cat's kiss," he heard Anna say, and his head deflated a bit, leaking consciousness down into his body, his arms, his legs. As he shrank, the room expanded again.

"Bumper," he said, and he bent down and scratched the round head and heard the small motor-boat once again burst into rumble. The cat had enjoyed his dinner, but the connection was more than that, too.

The purring grew because the room was so motionless and empty, so Anna-less and Snodo-less and Simba-less. Digger kneeled. Began petting the cat in long sweeping waves, head to tail, the short black hair rippling just a bit with each passing stroke. Beneath the black outer layer, Bumper's hair was touched with a red-brown fire, which showed up clearly in sunlight. In the kitchen's half-light, Digger had to picture the flames. Soon, the rumbling purr took over the room, an audio blaze devouring the dark, and as the little fire ate, Digger thought of Simba, how she had been a pilot light when his furnace had run nearly empty. The Lion Dog should be here and the White Unicorn, too, dancing about his legs, tails drumming, eyes beaming. Alone but for these ghosts, Bumper purred and purred as the outside world darkened and grew into nothing.

Digger stood again. How often had he stared at this ethereal scene out the window, beer in hand, all alone? Or almost alone. Anna had returned to his life, she had loved him again, and he had those facts. *Anna!* She was near now, but as he looked out at the lights across the water, each a pinprick like a lonely star, he knew that she was actually very far away, farther than any of those lights. *Humanity's stage set,* he thought, this view from his window, just one stage in billions of lives. If he ran beyond this little big stage, ran and crawled and just kept going, he still could not reach Anna now. Not yet, anyway. He could reach her now only through faith, and did he have enough of that? Had he ever had enough? *Probably not, and now?* Only an abyss of emptiness and a simmering desire for revenge.

The beer in his mouth was frothy and cold, sustaining. Digger's left temple itched, and he thought of the bullet, moving about to find a more comfortable nesting place, just as Snodo used to do on the couch and then in her little portable bed. He thought of her circling dance, poking at her blanket, and then flopping down. He thought of Simba, her big, goofy, wonderful grin. He rubbed his left temple. Time had him now, churning and mixing events. What happened in the past always seemed to pale compared to present experiences, yet Digger recognized that façade. Each past moment had been just as important as this present one, drinking a beer in the dark with a purring cat.

Anna would want to paint this scene, capture it. Once, he'd asked her why she didn't paint more often on the porch since the view out back was so beautiful, and she'd said that it was hard to paint outside, that the sunlight changed objects so much. In water, she'd said, a dark object's reflection will be a little lighter, a light object's a little darker. *Too dark to paint now*, Digger thought, and then he remembered a past conversation with her about growing old, probably from the past summer around one of their birthdays. Anna's came earlier, so he had no doubt asked her then whether she 'worried about' aging. He laughed now at her response then: "No, because women live much longer than men!" *Ah*, how wonderful it was to get busted by someone you trusted. And how he hoped that she were right.

The only sound was Bumper's purring. It rose and fell, no doubt in line with the cat's silent breaths. The kitchen window now looked like an abstract painting, motionless and soundless, nearly black with some subtle strokes for scrutiny. Just barely could he see the blue spruce, its limbs at rest, for even the usually incessant winds were now sleeping. Digger pictured them as winged serpents, coiled around trees and rocks, only softly in slumber, half lidded, ready for sudden flight. Winds were like that. Unpredictable. Matthew Diggerson finished the can of beer, thought about another. The lights from across the bay twinkled and became more defined on the ever darkening canvas. Fallen stars.

CHAPTER SEVEN

THE APPEALS OUTCOME

College writers need to know how to spot rhetoric, the art of persuasion, so they must learn about the three appeals: to ethos (the arguer's credibility), pathos (the audience's emotions), and logos (the argument's logic)—the triangle housing any argument. In their own academic writing, logos is most important, using clear points and valid evidence, both of which will highlight their own ethos, their credibility as writers. Pathos can be sprinkled into an essay's beginning and ending, for the audience's enjoyment, but emotions should play no part in a college report. Pathos must be carefully wielded in academia.

As winter took hold, Anna still slept, Digger at her side, reading, planning, staring at her still face. But as January drew to a close, he began the spring semester, which didn't really take off until February. Digger spent that snowy month in three places: OVC, Breezy Seas, the cottage. His four classes this young semester reminded him of the quartet from last fall, all eight courses being non-descript, no 'un-coachables' among the lot (apparently), a rarity. No students like George North all those years ago, and none like that Twitch character from several years past, and Digger wondered at times what that enthusiastic young man was doing today. Driving a sky-blue car? No, *silly!* Fall's students had been a fairly hard-working crew, and several 101ers had followed Digger into two of his spring 102 classes since, according to them, they liked his 'style,' how he let them work in groups and gave them early-exit opportunities (Earn and Learn) for many of the lesson plans. He appreciated the repeaters, who were usually leaders, helping each class to be successful. Their papers, too, tended to be good or even great, for what student would repeat a teacher who gave him or her C's?

After arriving at and when leaving Ocean View College each day, Digger repeatedly canvassed the Faculty Parking Lot for blue-blue cars, but so far he'd found mainly dark-blue Toyota Corollas or light-blue Priuses. The full-time faculty had their own lot, closest to the school, so he had to visit further parking areas to check the adjunct faculty and staff lots. In one, he'd discovered a bright blue Ford SUV (an EcoSport), which was small but definitely not little enough to be taken for a regular car, which is what the Candy Man claimed to have seen —the 'flash' of blue. Still, Digger had written down the lot location, the words 'Ford SUV,' and the license number. Then he'd immediately put a line through the information because the Ford showed no front-end damage. Guilt by color association—a gross generalization. Then, one lonely Friday late afternoon, Digger discovered a new lot, a small one hidden behind the Classroom Building on the south side of campus, and in it waited a dented old-model Hyundai Elantra, which was 'blue,' not dark or light, but *sky*. *Blue-blue!* Excited, he'd jotted down information and wondered how he could determine the owner, the 'driver.' Maybe he could ask colleagues about their cars ("What are you driving these days?"), but he'd quickly realized that such interrogations would be too obvious, an admission that he considered the person to be a possible wife-killer, an enemy. Would the police run the plate for him? Could he 'stake' the place out, as in the movies and on TV?

Why not? Twice during the next week, he'd waited along the little road outside that lot, quitting after half an hour or so each time, feeling impatient and silly (not to mention cold) as Time passed and nothing happened.

On the way to his office the following week, Digger felt as though he were in a parade due to the bystanders who seemed to line his route. First, he ran into (almost literally) Don Domberg, who emerged from the basement of the Administration Building, where Tutorial Services was housed. Don's appearance never changed, remained untouched by Time, probably because of his thick, sawed off beard, which made the man look old when he was young and vice versa now that he was old. "Digger!" the usually perky man said. "How's your pretty wife?"

The big smile and the word 'pretty' unbalanced Matthew Diggerson, temporarily made him picture Anna at home making pink cocktails instead of lying unconscious in a nursing home. Digger wondered what Don drove, probably an SUV, maybe that blue EcoSport.

"Anna's the same," he told his old friend, a colleague he'd been close to long ago but whom he'd seen less and less as the years passed. "How's your car?" Digger asked before he could stop himself.

"My car?" Domberg's smile almost left his face, but it peeked out still from the great brown beard. Digger thought of 'Just For Men' and wondered if his peer were fooling Time. "I drive an SUV, you know that. The headroom."

Don Domberg needed a vehicle that would fit his big head. That made sense. Digger smiled, his giggle having dried up at last. He hadn't giggled in two months. A seagull glided over the two men and screamed at them, making Domberg flinch and then laugh at himself. They looked up at the retreating bird, which looked like a flattened 'M' with a head. "Our mascot should be the 'Screaming Seagulls,'" said the bearded man, and Digger smiled and agreed. Then they told each other to "take care."

Next up, Digger stopped to speak with OVC's most prominent administrator, Omar Johns, probably the only person with a head larger than Don Domberg's. "Professor Diggerson," said the man, who always seemed to be in a hurry to be somewhere else. He stopped, though, and asked, "How are you? How's your wife?" When Digger gave quick answers, the administrator asked about the semester, wondered if he needed anything, any assistance from the administration. Digger didn't. Johns scampered off. Since nobody else popped out of the Administration Building—or perhaps to avoid them if they did—the composition instructor resumed his walk but stopped after passing the Psych Building, deciding to sit on William Watkins' bench, despite the chilly air. The wood-and-concrete two-seater boasted a little plaque that read, 'With thanks to Professor William Watkins,' and then gave the dates of his long toil at the school. A decade longer than Digger's time, but he'd nearly catch up with Watkins before leaving himself. *Six or seven more years.* Digger thought of adjuncts, their drifting off with no fanfare. Digger would probably get some sort of gold-plated clock and a little bon voyage party in the Admin Building. Maybe he'd even get a bench, but probably only if he paid for it. Digger sat down and sighed, which became a glowing tangible bubble for just a second in the February air. Behind the bench, a young maple tree offered thin, skeletal fingers to the sky.

Sitting alone in the cold made Digger feel self-conscious, and he wondered if anyone were watching him. Eliot used to look out his narrow office window quite often, but today Digger could see nobody peering from the Faculty Office Building, beyond which the Bay Bridge loomed. Digger stared at the great pylons and thought, "Oh, Danny, are you up there still? Did your soul float from the cold waters and get stuck on the cold skeleton of that bridge?" The teacher thought immediately of a little rhesus monkey, clinging to a metal mother, and with a sigh he blotted out that image, which had stuck to his conscience after seeing it in school. Was it high school or college? "Mental movies can destroy you," he concluded, and Anna's bed-ridden stillness flashed into view, as it did continually, both day and night. A decade past, she must have pictured him that way, but Anna had never lost faith. Digger had never really found any, accept in her and a little in Simba, in Snodo, in wild cats.

He pictured that blue Elantra, its dents, and decided to call the cop, Busher, and mention it. The cops would do nothing. What could he himself do? Could he call the DMV and pretend to be a policeman? *Silly!* Cold air rose up his legs and made him think of the bench. The famous (Digger often thought 'infamous') Professor Watkins was still among the living, so no ghost flitted about his modest memorial, which was hard and cold. Appropriate. Digger noticed the tentative approach of a handful of sparrows, creeping forward like neighbors who rarely visited, unsure of being welcomed. Unlike blue jays, who crashed in like tenement landlords, loud and demanding, sure of themselves.

"I have no bread crumbs," said Digger to the sparrows, who flew off together, synchronized but in various directions.

"Talking to yourself," said Lou Knightly, who'd appeared soundlessly, most likely from the FOB. Lou's strides could eat a lot of ground. "That's the first sign of insanity, you know."

Digger realized that the sparrows had fled because of this tall man, not because of his words. He smiled at the only peer who ever mentioned his books.

"I have reason to be crazy," he said, and the tall, thin man's smile flattened, his tongue passing over the lips.

"How's Anna?" he said.

"She's holding on, just like I did," said Digger, adding "but I hope she wakes up long before I did."

"She will, Digger," said Lou Knightly, an attitude that was often expressed.

Digger nodded. "How's married life?" he said, and the skinny man laughed, licked his lips once, then twice.

"Oh, it has its ups and downs, you know. You know how it is. Sometimes you just want to be alone."

Digger had never felt that way about Anna, but maybe that was due to their respect involving creativity, Digger's writing and Anna's art. They could be 'apart' in the cottage together. Digger kept these thoughts to himself, though, and just nodded in response to Knightly's words. "It can be hard," he finally said, thinking of 'life,' not 'marriage.'

"A-men!" said the tall man, who looked even more towering when viewed from a bench. Why, Lou even blotted out the Bye Bye Bridge! The middle of it anyway, for Lou was too skinny to obscure even a stop sign. The bridge seemed to pass through his stomach as though Lou Knightly were one mighty pylon, and Digger glanced up to see if gargoyles were perched on the man's boxy head. For a fanciful instant, he saw two of them, which transitioned quickly into Lou's ears. Digger would have giggled if the sound weren't lost so far within.

"Where are you off to?" he asked instead.

"Admin, another meeting. You never told me how many meetings the Chair needed to attend. Thanks a lot!" Lou laughed, licked his lips, and Digger smiled. Maybe Omar Johns had been hurrying away because he had to get back to meet with Lou. Picturing those two contrasting humans made Digger smile, a slight up thrust of his lower lip. When his colleague strode away up the sidewalk, eating space, Digger watched the man's shadow in chase. Distance made Lou's shadow longer and thinner than the man himself. Strange that Digger didn't even know what type of car Lou Knightly drove. Digger had suspected the usually jolly man in the past, and Lou had in fact ordered the Dream Board's removal. What had the short detective, Doyle, the only cop who'd actually helped Digger, once said about crime? *That strangers stole from you, but that family took your life? Theft versus murder.* Digger thought of the Writing Department 'family'—a dysfunctional clan! Lou Knightly, a back stabber? No, yet only a trusted person, a 'loved one,' could get close enough to wield a blade.

Inside the Faculty Office Building, Digger stopped to talk with one person whom he'd never suspected of any wrongdoing (other than excessive gossip), the department's secretary, Gloria Swanson, who asked about Anna and then about Digger himself. She had a look of concern on her face, and Digger knew that it was real, not a mask. Everyone said that Anna would awaken soon, a sentiment that began as a golden flash but that with repetition became greyer and darker. Although Digger knew that Anna 'had to' wake up, each passing day at her side took a little bite out of his optimism.

Perhaps that was the importance of faith, to be a shield against Time's little lunges.

Heading toward his office, Digger stopped at the open adjuncts' office door and looked in, finding just a seated Jay Moore, the Blinker. In the past several years, Jay seemed to have grown both shorter and wider, and looking at his seated peer, Digger thought, "This is how Lou sees the world, as 'down.'" Jay Moore was an aberration, the only 'hefty' composition teacher, many of whom were tall, too: Lou, Eliot, Paul Smith, Tobias. Two killers, a victim, and Lou. Even many of the women, chiefly Jolie, were thin, and as he traded pleasantries with the Blinker, Digger wondered if being skinny were a heavenly prerequisite for a college writing professor. Maybe to the angels hovering around the birth scene, all 'we' squawking infants clearly needed nourishment, soul food, and writing and reading provided it. It had for Digger, anyway. Sort of. Digger wondered what color car this part-timer drove.

"How does the semester look?" he asked instead.

"Oh, you know, Digger. They all look good at the beginning. Then they get a little monotonous."

"And then they end," finished Digger, and both men smiled. Digger wondered again about Jay's mode of travel. He decided to exit the scene and wished Jay good luck with the rest of the semester. Turning to leave, he swung back and said, "You drive a jeep, don't you, a nice green jeep? I saw it in the lot, nice vehicle."

Jay Moore blinked three times, as though he were trying to clear his eyesight. "You have me mixed up with some rich teacher," he smiled. "I drive an old Hyundai. I can't afford a jeep."

In his office, still in a bit of shock, Digger thought about Detective Busher and that blue-blue Elantra with the dents. Could it be Jay Moore's? Why would Jay smash his headstone and try to murder Anna? What could Jay have against him? Then again, what reasons did Eliot Gladstone have other than a character flaw, extreme envy over Digger's books, a jealousy connected to a distant past. All flaws had that link, that wire stretching into Time's shadows. *What appeared in Jay Moore's dark places?* wondered Digger, and then "Why does he blink so much?" Later, during his office hour between classes, Digger decided that he'd close his door and call the cop. What harm could it do? He'd mention the blue car and its license number, but not Jay Moore, not in a call from OVC anyway.

Preoccupied, Digger hardly remembered his first two classes and soon found himself alone again in his office. Gloria had gone either to a late lunch or home already, Jay Moore was no longer sitting in his shared office, and Digger felt the hallway's somewhat sad tone, an aura of loneliness and disconnection, a scene to two murders, too, though long ago now. When he called the OVPD number and gave Busher's extension, he was patched through to the detective. "I'm calling about my wife's, uh, accident, as you all call it," he said, hearing a noise that might have been a *hrumph*. "As you know, detective, I think that Anna was targeted, so I've checked all the lots around school, and in a lot for faculty and staff, I found a blue Hyundai Elantra with lots of dents. The guy at the candy store who saw the car said that it was blue, not dark blue or light blue, but blue-blue, a small blue car, and this Elantra with the front-end damage is that color. I have the license number and hoped that you could use it to, you know, 'run the plates.'"

Then he stopped, having basically summed up what he wanted to say, but the phone seemed dead. "Detective Busher?" he said.

"We can't tell you who owns that car. Privacy issues."

Liability issues, Digger thought instead, and then added, "Well, do you want the number anyway?" Silence.

"Let's have it," said the cop, adding another *hrumph* and then "Is that all?"

No, it definitely was not 'all,' but since Digger wasn't sure what else to add without beginning to yell, he said "BB, nine, one, one, two," and then, "By the way, my wife is still in a coma." Why not resort to pathos?

Busher said that he was 'aware of the situation' and ended the call. Digger sat and fumed a bit, thought that the cops were treating 'the situation' pretty poorly and in fact not at all. *Jay Moore's blue Hyundai Elantra*, the composition professor had decided, ignoring the phrase 'jumping to conclusions' because he wanted facts, proof, such as those dents, such as the killer himself. Digger imagined finding fibers—Anna's faux suede brown coat perhaps—in one of the dents. He began to obsess over fibers, over the Blinker's stupid face, his fat body, his dark motivations. Hadn't Moore been a realtor? Yes, and maybe he had a past, attacks against women, blow-ups of some sort. Maybe he'd been banished from the real estate business, his doings hushed up. *For liability reasons*! Digger let his thoughts romp about before logic crept back in. Lots of people had Hyundais, and the blue one was probably not Jay's and probably not even the one that had hit Anna. Maybe it had been an 'accident,' a drunk driver. There were certainly many of those around, lots more alcoholics than killers. Still, throughout his two afternoon classes, Digger thought of that car and pictured Jay Moore whenever a student blinked. And he saw that common bodily reaction everywhere, in every student, like a bunch of damn owls.

At 5:00, the outside world already darkening, Matthew Diggerson was glad to leave the office. He'd go home, feed Bumper, perhaps feed himself, and then head to Breezy Seas to see Anna, to sit by her bedside and just relax with her, to join her peaceful rhythm, to breathe.

The hallway was deserted except for George North, mopping halfway down the History Department corridor, which mirrored Humanities. Seeing the usual headphones on the janitor's head, Digger anticipated *hearing trouble* early in life for his one-time student, his and Tobias Mann's. Since George was so far down the opposite hallway, Digger waved, not expecting a connection other than that gesture, but George surprised him by stopping, taking off his headphones, and taking several steps forward. "I heard about your wife," he said.

Gloria! The good-natured woman was the conscience of the department, always knowing when a faculty's family member was ill or had passed, probably checking the paper's obituary for that very reason. "Yes," said Digger. "She's doing all right, hanging in there. She's a fighter."

"That's what the Hair said."

The Hair? "The hair?" said Digger.

The janitor laughed. "You know, the secretary with the big black hair. Gloria. She's about the only one who talks to me, besides you, but she likes to gossip. She'd talk with anyone. Sometimes I tell her I have to get to work! She told me about your father, too, how he died a long time ago in a car accident. You must not like cars much."

Round and round, life, and for a moment the composition teacher was swept back to a class featuring this fellow and his odd remarks, his strange jumps in coherence.

"My father," said Digger, but he didn't quite know what to say about that subject, how to finish the statement.

"The Hair said that 'fathers' were having a tough time this year." *Fathers?* Digger remembered something to do with 'father' talk—with Jolie? With Lou? With someone, but Digger's mind wasn't working too well these days. George seemed to think that his 'fathers' comment was amusing, or maybe the scrunched up look on the writing teacher's face ignited mirth.

"My father died in an accident," said Digger, adding "and so did my sister." Digger hadn't made George's connection about cars, but then he saw it. "Now, Anna. All *cars*. I think you're right, George." Then he wondered what the janitor drove.

But George *leaped* again. "Don't be so surprised, Professor. Just because I chose to do this job doesn't mean I'm a dummy. I get full health insurance, just like you, and a retirement plan, and year-round work, more year-round than you even since they have all those kid camps here all summer. Kids in groups giving speeches and learning how to be big-wigs. Giving me a job, though, with all their messes." George laughed and said, "Why, Professor Diggerson, we both rely on kids for our jobs!"

Digger had never heard such a soliloquy from this man, whom he'd somehow made defensive. Guilt erupted, so he said, "George, I envy you to be able to go home and leave work behind, not have any papers or lessons to worry about, or committees that need research. Oh, the committee work alone, George, you're not missing much!"

"We in Facilities have meetings, too," said George, adding "Plenty to discuss." Then he looked back down the History hallway as though someone had called. George would still be mopping these hallways years after Digger had retired, which was not far off, perhaps half a dozen years, and Digger pictured the other man in that future, alone in the hallway, just music for accompaniment. He thought of Bill Jacobs and John George and all the men who'd retired and would retire, going from not having enough time to being flush with it. What would he himself do? *Write?* But what? Billy D Wilder seemed played out after four books, yet that's how he'd thought after just two novels, then three, that he was done each time. Yet so far no new tale had progressed beyond a scattering of notes, no epiphanies wiggling around in his brain. Too much 'Anna' in there now, not to mention Snodo. Too many pale images, ghosts.

George turned back to Digger and said, "She'll be okay, professor. Your wife, everything will turn out all right."

This strange young man had done it again, the shift, leaving Digger to mumble his thanks as the other man returned to his monotonous work. Digger turned, too, but then George yelled out something. "What?"

"Life always *turns* out okay, professor, but sometimes you have to help with the *turning*!" Then the philosophical maintenance man slid his headphones up and turned his attention to the floor.

George was right, of course. What was that saying about luck, something about opportunity meeting preparation? being prepared. Perhaps Digger had been starting at the wrong point, looking for villains who arose in December, after Anna's attempted murder. What if the summer vandalism were the real starting point, or something even sooner. But what and when? All he had was the cemetery incident, all those broken stones, those names that littered his past, but who else's? George himself could be connected to Mann, albeit by a thin strand, but maybe that's where he had to start, with Tobias Mann, whose gravestone had been pulverized, repeatedly struck, much worse than the other ones. So seated alongside his sleeping love at Breezy Seas, Matthew Diggerson began to brainstorm, creating a new mind map, a visual representation of the known facts, with 'Tobias' in the center, not 'Anna,' who was always in the middle of his thoughts.

To his old colleague, he connected the words 'stone smashed completely.' Yes, what if Tobias were the kernel of it all? Clearly, Paul Smith had targeted him first, and Pinsky, although annoying, was more or less a secondary target, just like the Adams and Walt women, albeit a different killer. Could Eliot be tied to Tobias, beyond the obvious link as colleagues? Had they been friends? Digger couldn't really remember, had trouble picturing the two surly men standing together, so probably they hadn't been close. Still, no ideas were wrong when generating them, so Digger made lines and added thoughts. One line connected 'Tobias' to 'Eliot,' whose demon had been jealousy and its accompanying shadow, low self-esteem. Tobias showed neither of those weaknesses, so could the beginning of Eliot's demise also begin with Tobias Mann? All the madness branching from that one center?

Probably not, and what about that blue, dented Elantra? Was it Jay Moore's and how was the blinking adjunct connected to Tobias? Apparently, Digger himself had hired Jay several years after Tobias' death, so if those two men were connected, then

Digger's mind didn't contain that link. And what about his own place on the mind map? Eliot's link was more to Digger himself than to Tobias—at least directly. Yet Matthew Diggerson couldn't look past the Tobias' pulverized gravestone. The others were cracked, his old colleague's destroyed. Who else in their discourse community could be linked in a straight black line to Tobias? That's where the would-be murderer lurked, in that shadow cast by the past eighteen years. In the quiet of the Ward C room, the writing teacher knew what he had to do: go back in time.

At the cottage the next morning, Digger rifled through the Yellow Pages yet again and then dialed the number for 'Tobias Mann,' not to contact the dead, of course, but the one left behind, the wife. He had some questions. Looking at the microwave's clock, which read 10:04, Digger wondered what Amy Mann would be doing and how he should begin the conversation. Why was he calling? That would be her first thought, so what would he say? An appeal to help, perhaps, since most people felt propped up by that attitude, humble and in need of assistance. Yes.

Her phone rang four times before the click and a woman's voice, a croaking "Yes?" that made Digger think, "Is she drunk? Ten a.m. intoxicated?"

"Amy, this is Matthew Diggerson, a voice from the past, is this too early to call?" Amy Mann or whoever, the croaker, said nothing, and Digger thought that maybe he had talked too fast. "Amy, this is Matt Diggerson, Tobias' old colleague, and I'm calling to get some help."

"Matt Diggerson? Why are you calling?" The voice slurred and croaked, and Digger thought that maybe the woman had suffered a stroke. How old would she be now? *Old!*

"Amy, I need your help. I'm calling about the vandalism of our stones from the summer, the gravestones that were toppled over, our stones."

"Our stones? Are you dead, Matthew Diggerson! Am I on the phone with the Great Beyond?" Then the old lady laughed and laughed. Digger held the landline phone away from his head, but the mirth bubbles kept falling out of the handle. Amy Mann laughed for at least ten seconds straight. Then she stopped abruptly and said, "How can I help you, Matthew Diggerson, Tobias' *old colleague?*"

Digger felt a need to both hang up and explain, choosing the latter. "I know, it sounds odd, but I have a gravestone already. My wife purchased our headstone, very early, I know, but she wanted to get it, and she designed the picture herself, with our dogs and some trees and a pair of deer, and …"

"Fascinating, Digger, but I'm sure that you didn't call me to describe your tombstone." Then she laughed again, a couple of barking 'Ha's.' She seemed drunk.

"No, but did you know that your stone wasn't the only one vandalized? What did the cemetery people tell you about your stone?"

Silence, which Digger took as the croak-laugher's thinking, a good sign. Then Amy Mann said, "Some guy called and said that our stone had been 'damaged.' *Damaged!* The damn thing had been pulverized into dust! But he said 'damaged' and for me 'not to worry.' He said it would be fixed, 'free of charge,' by the fall. Then he said something like, 'It will be brand new then' and maybe 'for your viewing pleasure,' but that doesn't sound right, does it? Did he say 'viewing pleasure'?"

Amy Mann seemed to be talking to herself now. Digger said, "Our stone—Anna's and mine—was also broken, as were a handful of others, one being Dan Pinsky's. He was killed by Paul Smith. Too." Digger had added the latter word separately, as though it were a new statement, and he waited for that information to pass through the lines and into the widow's head. *Into the Widow's Head.* It sounded like a murder mystery title.

"Paul Smith," announced the croak-laugh-drinker. "What's he up to these days?"

Digger hesitated, wasn't sure if Amy had actually asked a question or just used one to mask a statement. Then she said, "Huh!"

"He's still in jail. I asked about him, asked the cops, and Paul's been accounted for." He didn't tell her that Paul Smith was no longer in a maximum-security prison, that his age and 'good behavior' had improved his daily living situation.

"Asked the cops," said Amy Mann, who seemed to be ruminating on those words.

"Because of the stones, the people involved, I thought of Paul Smith first, so I asked about him." Digger wasn't sure if what he'd just said was even true, but it sounded right. Then he added, "If Paul had had a son, even a daughter, I'd have wondered about them, too."

"Wondering about sons and daughters, that's something that I understand, Matthew Diggerson. Do you have any lovely offspring?" When Digger said that he didn't, the woman replied, "How sad!" but it sounded sarcastic. Digger thought about Tobias' son, what was his name? What kind of car did he drive?

"How are your kids?" he asked to get the mother talking, to find a pathway to a blue car, another one besides the Elantra.

"Oh, Richard is doing quite well, Mr. Big Insurance man. He makes piles of money off of other people's anxiety." She stopped, as though awaiting some reply, but Digger was thinking about insurance and real estate, a possible connection between buying houses and insuring them, between Jay Moore's past and Tobias' son, Richard. "And Pam, Pam," continued Amy Mann, "what can I say of Pam? She never visits, so I can say nothing of Pam." Dead stop again.

"This might sound strange, but do you, or Richard, or did Tobias ever know a man named Jay Moore?"

"Jay Moore," said the woman, repeating the name a couple times as though tasting it, trying it out. "No."

"No?"

"No!"

"You've never heard of Jay Moore?"

"Who the Hell is Jay Moore!"

"Nobody," said Digger, adding, "Just a lead I had, but nobody, apparently. Let me ask another question. Had you received last summer, or have you recently, any sort of threats?" He'd certainly mangled that question.

"Threats!"

"Phone calls, letters, vandalism at your house, anything strange?"

"Just this call, Matt Diggerson. This is pretty strange, wouldn't you say?"

Digger chuckled at that, but mainly to placate the other human. "Nobody else has called and then hung up, that sort of thing?"

"Just the telemarketers, Mr. Digger. You know how they are, those robo-calls, whoever picks up first has to wait to hear the fake human."

Digger knew, but he didn't want to go down that road, complaints about robo-calls. "Nothing vandalized at your home, your bushes maybe or your car?"

"I don't pay much attention to the shrubbery, Digger, and nobody has done a thing to my car."

"What are you driving these days?" Digger asked, the question trailing off because it seemed so manipulative.

"Same as always, a Volvo. Did you want to get a new car, is that why you're asking, Digger? Well, I'd definitely suggest a Volvo."

Digger chuckled again, for the same reason. "Have the police contacted you?"

"About my Volvo? Ha-ha, Ha-ha!" Her laugher sounded like gun shots, the violence and sudden echo. This call had been a waste of time.

"About the cemetery vandalism. I'm asking because my wife was struck by a car, and the police think it was a drunk driver, just an accident, but after the cemetery vandalism, I'm not so sure. That's why I'm asking all these questions. I'm looking for connections."

"Was your wife struck by a Volvo?"

Digger closed his eyes and tried to quiet the pounding blood.

"Digger?" called the woman. "Matthew Diggerson, are you there?"

"Anna was hit by a blue car, but nobody knows the type, the brand."

"My Volvo is black. I certainly didn't use it to run over your wife. Are you married now? You must be if she was run over. I remember that you were married but that your first wife ran away, or something like that."

"She came back," said Digger. "I'm married to the same woman, to Anna, and right now she's lying in a coma due to that blue car. That's why I'm calling, Amy. The cops won't do anything. They don't see any connections. They're blind!"

"Maybe there are no connections, Matthew. Have you considered that? Sometimes life just does not connect."

Digger wondered what the widow meant, but he didn't ask. "I'm sorry to bother you, Amy, and maybe you're right. Maybe there are no connections. But I think there are. Are you sure that you don't remember anything odd these past few months, like car tires flattened or writing in your driveway, anything?" Digger pictured a chalk warning: 'Never Forget!' But *forget* what? The desecrated tombstones suggested that someone could not forget something, and that was the key! The *something*, but what?

"You'll have to search some other shadows to find your villains, Digger. I find mine in scotch; that's a fine place to look." When Digger failed to respond quickly enough, Amy Mann left him with some advice before abruptly disconnecting: "About second marriages, Matthew, they never work. Sooner or later, the two people remember what drove them apart the first time, and then history repeats."

Digger was about to thank her sarcastically for her advice when he heard the metallic disconnection. He looked at his mind map and made a line from 'Tobias' to the word 'Amy,' and from there he added lines ending with 'Richard, Insurance Agent,' 'Pam, never visits,' and 'alcoholic, scotch.' Each of these lines ended with a dead end, most likely, but then he added another from 'Richard' to 'Jay Moore—job connection?' As he always told his students, no thoughts were 'wrong' when generating ideas. Yet all his lines led just to one center, his own name, or perhaps to all those other names connected to Ocean View College, for didn't they all connect? Well, not to the Walt woman's stone in Ocean View Cemetery, and not to Anna's 'accident.' Only his name connected to those two lines. Red herrings? Perhaps this villain, this new Paul Smith and Eliot Gladstone, was laying out breadcrumbs on a false trail. Perhaps this killer understood rhetoric. Digger's mind map, his creative visualization, had formed chaos, exactly where Matthew Diggerson now toiled.

He needed to do work in the 'real' world, to escape for a bit the fictional one, the world of possibilities only, the land of sledgehammers and deadly blue cars. His publisher, Pat Covington, had recently reminded Digger to spend more time on Facebook promoting his books, an action required by his contract. Pat had not mentioned the latter, but Digger often fixated on that fact and felt guilty about not going on social media, which he didn't enjoy, to put it mildly. Perhaps luckily, the composition teacher had papers to do that weekend, many essays landing from cyberspace, and he'd grade them on his laptop at Breezy Seas, with Anna. Facebook would have to wait, all those strangers left hanging for the latest Billy D Wilder news. Instead, Digger would read Anna some of his students' good sentences and maybe some mangled ones, some silly proofreading errors, the way the curmudgeon Bill Jacobs used to do, posting them on the adjunct office board. Digger had never forgotten Bill's favorite student faux pas: 'Sometimes I take my parents for granite.' Although the man had been too negative too often, that mistake was classic. Then he remembered the word "Hack" from a *fan* on his website, a condemnation echoing from the past. He'd have to check that neglected site for any recent messages.

Anna slept, and seated alongside her bed, Digger thought, "The artist slept, the writer wept." But he was dry-eyed, as usual, the walls held. *Good fences made good neighbors* even when the 'neighbors' were in a person's own head. It was late, quiet. Digger had checked his 'author' website, found no new messages, and then graded over a dozen essays, and he was slumped back in the chair, which was always soft and comfortable until it wasn't, usually after a couple hours. *Neighbors*. Graham had said that he'd keep an eye on 'the cat,' but what did that mean? How would that help? Digger wondered about Donna, Graham's wife. Where the hell was she? Digger hadn't seen the woman in months, several of them, but that was less odd perhaps because Graham was the one Digger talked to most, over the fence, Donna only when she trailed out of the house to see what the two men were discussing. If he had to pick Donna out of a lineup, Digger might even have a little trouble. He felt a little guilty about Bumper, whom he'd definitely neglected this winter, but the black Tom cat didn't seem to hold grudges, just greeted him whenever he came home, early or late, and purred away at the present. That cat, there was something so peaceful and all knowing about it. If Bumper were the character in a movie, he'd probably end up being some celestial visitor, maybe even an angel. If the cat were to walk across the air to him one night, Digger would hardly have been surprised.

But Bumper must be cold; it was cold out. And getting late. And Anna wasn't going anywhere, not at the moment. Digger looked at his wife and watched the slow, soft breaths move the flat white sheet a bit. Her vitals were *good*, and according to Nurse Addie, she was maintaining her weight, and that was very good. Soon Anna would awaken, but that moment didn't appear to be tonight.

Digger closed his laptop, got up from the chair, groaned twice because his knees hurt, especially the right one. He was getting *old*, and that thought made him think of his mother. Jean's attitude had seeped into her son, inevitable perhaps. Standing, staring down at Anna, Digger felt the room take on a golden glow, as though it were a small universe hurtling through a dark expanse, and he realized that Anna would love to paint this scene. He could hear her now, talking about acrylic paint, how a spray bottle was needed so that the paint would mix and flow since it dried up so quickly. She would want 'warm and cool' colors. With acrylics, "you don't get unwanted paint mixes, such as a tree's leaves into the sky," he could hear her say. She had told him that the pallet needed to be close to the painting "so that you could compare the colors more easily and clearly." She loved to paint, and that thought led to Snodo. She was going to turn a photo of Snodo into a picture, with 'warm and cool' colors, she had mentioned it to him more than once. Digger wanted that painting with a fierce desire, so strong that he felt as though he could focus it into being himself. He did so, every night, as Time held him in its soft, nocturnal paws, talons retracted until the sunrise.

On the drive home, Digger thought of the warm feeling of Anna's forehead on his lips, which still seemed to be tingling. Warmth, that was a good sign. Her vitals were *good*. Still out on the man road, when he saw an incomplete square sign for a new store, another coffee shop, no doubt doomed to failure (hadn't there once been a coffee shop in that very same building?), Digger thought suddenly of his Dream Board, of the pale square on the wall outside his office. Why worry about that? Who really cared? Nobody, not even him anymore. Diana Pell was gone, no more poems, and even Jolie's music seemed to have dried up. Digger thought of that famous poem, of the 'raisin in the sun.' Had janitor George tossed the board or kept it, and why did that thought appear? A vision of George North sifting through the Dream Board and reading. It made no sense. As a student, George hadn't seemed to enjoy reading, and as the janitor, he never said anything about books, except perhaps some sarcastic comment. Neither did Digger to him, though, so who knows? Maybe George had even read Digger's books, and if so wouldn't that raise his OVC readership by 33 percent? Lou and Gloria and George. His three fans. Matthew Diggerson almost giggled. He thought again of his website fan, of the word "Hack!"

Sometimes Lou Knightly wished that he still lived alone, especially those nights when he and Angela would bicker over something that seemed of paramount importance to her and of little consequence to him. "You are turning mountains into molehills," he'd declare, but that fact didn't improve the woman's vision, not with those *blinders* on. What had it been tonight? He couldn't even remember the 'molehill.' Now he was thinking about Digger's old Dream Board, how he'd had the janitor remove it from the wall since nobody was adding anything to it and since, he argued, it had become a fire hazard. The latter argument had worked immediately. *Nothing like a little litigation!* But he'd felt guilty, too, because the Dream Board had been a good idea at one point, and Digger's books shouldn't negate his own efforts, his own career. Maybe married life would give him some plot to explore. It had certainly added both light and darkness to his existence, and isn't that what Digger was always going on about, that life was invisible without both sides, that the darkness was needed to stress the light? Something like that, something poetic and artistic sounding.

Could murder mysteries hold poetry and art? Lou Knightly had to admit that Digger's books did, four of them, four 'novels,' if a book from that genre could be described that way. *Yes*, those books were an accomplishment and should be celebrated, but not with a Dream Board. *No*, he'd do something more, *a display case*. Other buildings showcased faculty printed efforts, didn't even the History Department have one down their hallway? Yes, a display case, and Digger could add his books and a little card saying when they were published, and others could add their efforts, too. Lou tried to think of those, couldn't muster any up beyond Diana Pell's poems. *A ghost's poetry*, that sounded worthy of print itself. His own editorials, *no*, they weren't 'scholarly' enough, but maybe he'd write one. That was the answer, wasn't it? He would publish a piece and feel good, and then even his little spats with Angela wouldn't seem so important. Definitely, publishing a peer-reviewed article was the answer. The question was 'about what?'

How had Digger even thought up enough stuff for four books? They weren't short books, either, although the first was a little skimpy. Digger had said that the writing got easier, that once a writer built a fictional world, he could just walk around in a scene to get ideas. Maybe that was true. Digger's marriage seemed idyllic, too. *Some sonofabitches just had it all*, but then Lou Knightly remembered Anna's accident, her current state, a coma. Should he visit her, maybe he and Angela both could drop by? Maybe Angela would see how good she had it, seeing Anna's lying there. At Breezy Seas, wasn't that where she was? Didn't Digger always talk about Breezy Seas? That's where he'd been, *Breezy Seas*. Kind of a *silly* name! But all those places had emotional names, like Whispering Woods or Sheltered Hollow or some such rot. What was the one his mother had landed in? *The Beachwood Arms!* Where all the royals ended, as long as they had insurance, anyway. Lou checked himself, recognized the dark path he was treading. That argument with Angela, its tentacles still out and pulling him down. Digger's display case, the department's case, that would be nice, and the newlywed thought about a scholarly article, about a topic. Peer Reviews, everybody loved them— *except students*. How many times had he asked students directly about peer reviews and discovered that they didn't feel comfortable writing comments on other people's papers and couldn't understand the criticisms planted on their own? Yes, *peer reviews*. He'd have to do some research, see who else had waved a yellow flag over this most common of his peers' lesson plans. Maybe his article could cause a sensation.

Lou Knightly's thoughts ping-ponged about, making him feel more connected to the world, less alone in the night. He decided to bring Angela a nice cup of coffee in the morning.

CHAPTER EIGHT

THE WRITING TYPES OUTCOME

College assignments tend to fit into two genres, two types: essays and reports. Both almost always have the same explanatory purpose, the straight forward communication of information, yet each offers its own characteristics, its typical elements. While 95% of college papers will fall into one of those genres (mainly essays), other writing types might appear, such as observation papers (in Education, usually), description ones (in Art, most likely), narratives (in English at times), or arguments (most often in writing classes themselves). And students will often study different writing genres, from poetry to scholarly articles, all offering myriad elements to be learned and sometimes even performed.

The dented blue Elantra moved around, sometimes even appearing in student parking lots, but Digger realized that those moves just meant that the driver had trouble finding a space. That probably meant that he (or she) didn't teach 8 a.m. classes since plenty of parking existed then, or at least it used to when Digger taught an early schedule. He'd memorized the license plate, too: BB9112. How easy was that? Bilbo Baggins and then the two 1's, the slatted eyes of the devil! Just the '9' and '2' were a challenge, and the others stood out so much that remembering the beginning and ending numbers didn't really matter. Then Digger thought of '911,' the distress call, another easy memory device. He wondered if Detective Busher had bothered to 'run' the license plate. Probably *not!* Matthew

Diggerson had rarely felt more alone, more angry, more driven. Every day, he kept an eye out for the car's owner.

After six weeks, the spring semester had progressed into March, and still he'd discovered nothing, still Anna slept, still Nurse Addie complemented her 'good vitals,' still Digger went home for just two basic reasons: to feed Bumper and to sleep. His nearest neighbors appeared to have vanished (a vacation in March? Normal for college writing teachers, but not for other professions), and the maples in the next neighbor's yard all sprouted red tips, making Matthew Diggerson wonder if all birth required a down-payment of crimson blood. And he wondered if he had as of yet paid that price.

Spring Break was coming, and the composition instructor had to admit that he welcomed the week 'off.' A few students had turned into possible un-coachables, those who wouldn't listen, and Digger knew that grades had caused the change. Grades were emotional. Although he urged students to look at those capital letters as friends, as guides, he realized that some students viewed a 'C' as their being *average* humans. Even a 'B' could vex a student who considered him or herself to be *great*. Easier for these late teens to blame him than themselves, so the un-coachables wouldn't use his models, checklists, and other materials, but instead   stick to their own beliefs and habits, even when those choices were blatantly illogical, such as beginning an essay with its thesis or using long 'ing' subjects in every other sentence or something even more obvious, such as putting a period before a citation instead of after it, allowing the citation to float away from its sentence, over and over, despite Digger's reasoning, the same mistakes every time. Some students put up fences, *good fences, bad neighbors!* Digger could never fix this problem, these students, because their disconnections stretched into the unknown past, stunted roots in rocky gravel, stone attitudes, human nature. Who could possibly understand them? George North had been like that a couple decades past, as though he weren't in college to gain knowledge, but to show it.

He'd suspected one un-coachable early on but had wished away the possibility. During the first class, the student had declared that her name was 'Kaitlyn,' not 'Kate' or 'Katie,' but 'Kaitlyn,' full stop. *Uh-oh*, Digger had thought, for that refusal to be shortened was sometimes a sign of an un-coachable, a chin up to informality, a challenge but not a connection. Every moment of life as a challenge. Digger had wondered in that moment if that's how Eliot Gladstone had felt, and what about a poor, isolated student like Danny Jones, the wide-eyed ghost from the Bay Bridge? What about himself? In his feelings of disconnection from so many colleagues, was Digger challenging humanity? No, maybe *surviving* it, but not challenging. Not like Kaitlyn, a 'B' writer who considered herself an 'A' and who scoffed at any teacher dumb enough not to see the excellence in her prose. Why were these disconnecting students often females? Probably, in general girls earned better grades than guys in high school and simply expected that pattern to continue in college. An unfortunate pattern. Just as a crowd of peaceful protestors sometimes held looters, a classroom of learners hid one or two students who considered themselves already to have reached the apex of knowledge. Human nature.

Yet Digger hardly worried about Kaitlyn and the few other students who seemed to be turning from his guidance. The past would swallow them soon enough, as it did everyone and everything else. *Anna!* That word and image was just about all

Digger thought about. Even the image of Snodo's bright eyes was dimmed beneath the word 'Anna.' And he was also obsessed by a blue-blue car called an Elantra.

On the Friday before Spring Break, Digger received a gift, a momentary distraction, when he discovered a two-shelf, glassed-in display case outside the corridor to the Humanities Department, and seeing it brought the first real smile to his face since Anna's 'accident.' *Lou,* he thought. *Lou did this*. And as if on cue, the tall man popped out of his room (Diana's old office), strode up the hallway, and said, "I see you've seen your display case, Digger."

"Mine?"

"Well, mostly yours, but with this display case, the rest of us will have motivation to catch up. I've already begun a scholarly article, about peer reviews, and I need to get the publisher info from you, the one you mentioned using."

"I'll email you the link and the editor's name," said Digger, still looking at the clean, shiny case, happy for a moment. He'd realized that his mysteries had distanced him from humanity, not drawn him closer to it, as he'd always imagined being an author would do. At OVC, he actually felt *less* liked now, but he'd recently understood that that opinion had probably always been the case, been *fact,* such as during all those informal hallway conversations, all those faculty meetings, even the occasional sightings outside Ocean View College. Nobody *really* like him, not outside his home and his dwindling extended family. A sad epiphany. But this display case made a difference. Maybe he'd been wrong. Lou seemed to appreciate his friendship. *Friends versus strangers*, Digger thought, but he stopped that view, that attitude, from forming.

Lou was smiling. "Get me your books, Digger, and I'll put them right on the top shelf. Maybe you could create a little card that describes each one, and add the copyright date, too. Let's get some color in here. I'm going to contact Diana Pell's son. Remember him from that Christmas party? I'm going to add her last book of poetry, maybe a couple of the others, too, just to give the case some substance. Your book covers will add some nice color."

"When did you do this, Lou? I'm surprised that Administration footed the bill."

"You wouldn't be wrong, old friend. This one came from some storage room. Last week I talked to Omar Johns about it. I argued that a writing department needed to celebrate its writers, that it only made sense, and Omar hemmed and hawed and said that he'd do what he could. You know Omar, he's been here forever. He'll never leave his leather armchair and alumni cocktail parties, either. Omar's round head will be here until long after he's dead, calling alumni and begging for donations. You'd think that a student's coming to this school and paying for classes would be enough, but administrators like Omar just keep dipping into the well."

Digger, still smiling at the case, said, "That's the way life works, I guess. Nothing's ever what it seems."

Lou smiled, too, and then licked his lips once. *He wants to eat the world*, thought Digger, but not unkindly. "Anna will really be happy about this case, thanks a lot for your efforts!" he said.

Later on, in his office between his pair of Monday, Wednesday, Friday classes, the hallway's solitude began to creep back in, as it always did in the afternoons, especially on Fridays. Digger looked out his narrow window. The library wasn't doing much of a business this day, and then he remembered why: Spring Break. At least half the student body had already jumped ship. In his 2:00 and 3:00 classes, Digger would be lucky to have a handful of students.

Due to the empty campus and the office hour's silence, the glow from the new display case had dimmed a bit. Digger had forgotten to ask Lou about his 'new' wife, Angela. And when had he last discussed anything with Todd or Jeff? Even the adjuncts, Digger hadn't stopped and gone into their office for weeks. Jay Moore was no doubt innocent of everything but excessive blinking, and had Digger ever said a thing to the two new part-timers, Ben Something and 'Liz' George, the name he could never forget? He thought about his colleagues and what they knew about each other. Just the *resumes*, really. Grad school, field of study, family situation (*sometimes*). Again, he thought of Todd, Midwestern Todd, the drawl, but nobody's image of a gunslinger. Was Todd married? No, and what about Jeff? He called himself a 'confirmed bachelor'—when he said anything at all. When had Digger last seen Jeff, let alone stood and spoken with him? And Jolie? Prickly, undiplomatic (rare for a pedagogue), opinionated. Who would have hired Jolie? Not Tobias, definitely, but perhaps Gwena had. Yes, Gwena would have looked past the fire to see the flame in Jolie, the potential behind the thorns. Had Jolie reached that potential? Digger missed Gwena Schmidt. He'd actually been to her house, been invited to dinner, and once he'd gone to a party at Tobias' and not so long ago to Diana Pell's, as Lou had referenced earlier. When had he ever invited colleagues to the Cottage? Digger knew that he was as much to blame as any of his peers for their superficial 'friendships.'

Maybe not *as much.* Digger thought about his first book, *Composition Murder,* how happy it had made him, but how when he told any peer about it, the person would switch the subject to his or her own writing project, deflecting an actually published piece for one that didn't even exist—*fictional fiction.* Even when he asked colleagues about their classes, about 'what they did in class' that day, even after he listened to all the long details and justifications for the great teaching moments that had taken place, did they then ask him about his classes? He thought of Willy Loman, his favorite anti-hero, and of his wife Linda's words at the salesman's funeral: "Attention must be paid." A universal truth. Digger pictured the display case down the hall, visually added his four books, and was nourished. That *was* 'attention,' and Anna would be happy. Thoughts were like drugs, he realized. Glancing out his office window, the library clocks declared that he had fifteen minutes before his next-to-last class (the right tower said thirteen minutes). The spring semester was almost half over. Digger jumped slightly when he heard a voice raised in emotion.

"Ohhhh! What's this?"

Jolie Matterson, *uh-oh!* Digger got up, traversed the hallway, and stood with Jolie looking down at the empty case. "Where are your books?" said Jolie.

"I just found out about the case, too, and I don't have copies in my pockets."

"Touché, Digger. Don't get touchy. I just couldn't picture anything else but your books going in here. Maybe Diana's poetry, but is this case for posthumous writers?"

"It's a celebration of our writing; Lou got it put here. It's for all of us."

"Well, Admin's full of surprises, aren't they! Now I guess I'll have to use Spring Break to write. Mary will just have to amuse herself. I'll be busy, and I won't be able to visit my loving brother, oh!"

"That's the spirit," Digger said, but he wasn't sure what the woman's 'spirit' actually was, probably sarcastic. Not even *probably*. They bid each other a fond week off, Jolie's words trailing her as she left. *She likes to get in the last word,* Digger thought, trying to picture family gatherings at the Mattersons. What had she said about her father? Was he still alive? They knew nothing about each other really, just resumés.

Alone again in his office, Digger imagined inviting Jolie and Mary to the Cottage. *Hard to envision that foursome.* Anna would make it work, though, and definitely Lou and Angela would be fun. Probably, anyway, for he'd never met Angela. Digger made a pact with his own introverted nature: if (when) Anna awakened and when she got better, they'd invite colleagues over for dinner. Salmon, baked potatoes, asparagus. Maybe even host a party and not do any cooking. Just booze and snacks. Even Jolie would agree to a party, but then he couldn't remember having seen her at Diana Pell's house, a week or so before another colleague, the jealousy-twisted Gladstone, had hurled the poetess down the stairs and into eternity.

He'd waited for her in a lot near the Faculty Parking because the school had *no cameras out here*, none that he knew of. If the woman went onto any main road, he'd have to let her go because he couldn't risk being seen behind her. His plans would no doubt allow a witness or two, depending on where she stopped—if she did. If not, he'd simply have to try again.

"If at first you don't succeed, right, Dad!" As he followed the Prius, he expected to succeed because this woman seemed like the type to stop and buy things, like Vegan sandwiches and sour tasting wine, or maybe little whips and other kinky lesbian devices. In her light-blue Prius, this one would never simply drive home and have a nice pasta dinner in front of the TV. Nothing simple about bitches like her, the stains they left on the past, indignities on the soul, with their offhand comments and pinched faces. Too important to sacrifice even minutes from their days. Too bad erasing her had to be so quick, but the other plans had all seemed too risky. Diggerson would have approved the time he'd put into organizing this correction. Lists, a table of pros and cons for each idea, even a flow chart —the whole shebang! That was a funny word, 'shebang.' Seemed appropriate, though.

Oh, this was it! Wouldn't you know it, *Target*! How fitting in a way, although she wasn't his main target, he'd hit that, and did he have another main target? He thought of his sister and then again of the nasty woman in his sights. Of all the nasties, this one was the nastiest. Always arrogant, *dismissive*, worse even than his father! *Ah, Dad*, crackered already, and now for some more erasing! The bitch's Prius had pulled into the megastore's giant parking lot, which was packed as always. With any luck, the nasty woman would have to park way back here, without all the cameras perched like vultures. Big Brother! More like *Fat Father*, but not out in the concrete sea, in the deep water, with *us sharks*. The *target!* What was that word for 'happy coincidence'? Zippidy? *Zippidy-do-dar* or some such nonsense. From going to Target to being the target. *Zippity-dippity-do-dar-day!*

When Jolie Matterson climbed out of the Prius, she felt her back muscles ache. She was *getting old*, she knew, but she blamed it on the little car's sunken seats. Maybe she'd get an assed-sized pillow in Target, too, along with her list of 'needs.' She sensed and half saw the blue car's approach behind her, but it had plenty of room to pass by. She headed toward the store, heard a motor rev, and turned to see what the *idiot* was doing.

She never did see. The car knocked her down, rolling at a fairly slow but steady pace, and her head slammed into the pavement. *What the!* The bastard had run her over! Groggy, she started to raise her head when she heard that revving noise again, and a second or two after that point, all of the long-time composition professor's earthly senses ceased to function.

It was *easy*, it was as inconspicuous as possible, as slow as could be. He'd knocked her down and then reversed, finishing the job. *Shebang!* After he felt the double thumps and continued back a ways, he turned to see that the woman's crumpled body had been flipped over and that a fountain or red was issuing from her open mouth. *So much blood!* How could it continue to sprout out like that? He pictured blood coating his car's belly and oozing from the tire treads. It made him momentarily nauseous. Got to *get out* of here!

Panicked, he sped away but calmed himself down after several seconds. Nobody had seen a thing, and he couldn't spot any cameras anywhere. *Probably just in front of the doors*, and he'd never driven by those. *Think, think!* He had to get his car washed! He pictured blood trailing from his tires and leading to him, wherever he went, a long trail of that *bitch's blood*. The way it fountained from her mouth, a geyser! He'd never forget it; it would haunt him forever. But he knew just where to go, to that do-it-yourself car wash before the highway. As he drove, he wondered if he'd gone too far, if the haunting were 'karma.' The other run-down, Diggerson's wife's, had been exhilarating, sort of fun, but not horrible like this, not haunting. Maybe that was because this one was definitely dead. He'd seen the blood, the way it just flew up and away, like a damn geyser. She'd be empty by now.

At the car wash, he put in his quarters and concentrated on splashing the tires and underbelly; then he moved the car up a few feet, put in more quarters, and washed it again. The water and suds revived him, made him feel fresh, and blew away the blood from his mind. His car was clean again, totally blood free, but maybe it was time for a new one. If his father's damn will would just pass through probate. If his sister were holding it up—*Beverly*—he'd definitely have to go find her and do some more cleaning. That thought buoyed him, kept the ghost of Jolie Matterson at bay, but that spewing *fountain*! He just couldn't quite erase it. Did it mean that he should stop these endeavors or increase them?

On the first day of Spring Break, Digger read the administration's email about Jolie Matterson's shocking death while seated next to Anna at Breezy Seas. He was dumbstruck; he'd just talked with her. He must have been the last person to speak with Jolie, and he tried to remember what they said, hoped he'd ended the conversation with something nice, as though that mattered. Near the email's end, he got another jolt, for Jolie had been run over by a car. His first reaction was "Yes!" because his suspicions had been proven true, but that feeling fostered a bubbling of guilt. For him to be right, Jolie had paid the price. But it wasn't 'being right' that mattered to

Digger, it was having Anna's 'accident' investigated the way it should have been right from the start: as 'attempted murder.'

"Now we'll get some action," he said to Anna as he fumbled for her phone and then dialed the OVPD number, long since memorized. After being connected to Detective Busher's extension, Digger learned right away that Busher had been assigned to this new hit-and-run, too, but then the man doused him completely by saying, "Looks like another drunk driver. A witness said that the car drove erratically."

"What car?" said Digger.

"The blue one," said the cop, then, "Oops. Disregard that information, professor."

Digger felt the prickling of righteous anger, a flame that not even the incongruously human sound "oops" could dispel. "How can I disregard such a prime piece of evidence, detective? Blue, a *blue* car! How many blue cars are out there, anyway, running over people?"

"Blue is one of the most common car colors, professor. Black and blue."

"So you don't think that my colleague's death was murder? You think it was another *accident*, another involving a *blue* car? You believe in coincidences like that? Was it a blue *Elantra*, by the way?"

The man had no more words, not for Digger at any rate. The writing professor had gotten the *bum's rush* again. After the call, Digger sat still with his eyes closed and tried to calm himself down. How much proof did the Ocean View cops need before they saw reality? He picked up his notebook, turned it lengthwise, and jotted down the facts in the form of a flow chart, left to right. He started with the vandalism at the cemetery, the names desecrated, Tobias Mann's first, and then the facts around Anna's being hit, and now Jolie's, the comparisons. Then he contemplated his visual and tried to be objective. Was it a strong case? No, even Detective Doyle might have disagreed with Digger's conclusions, yet it was a *case*.

Digger closed his eyes again and rested, thought about Jolie, took a power nap, and an hour later he looked at his flow chart again. Yes, something was definitely there, so he called Detective Busher back. "Detective Busher," he said. I'm sorry to take up your time." He wasn't sorry. "I just wanted to cover some of the facts, if you have a little time." He'd have to make the time.

But then the other man cut in: "Professor, we've released the witness' photo to the news outlets. You can probably see it online now. If you have any further information, feel free to call back."

Digger held the phone to his head even though the cop had obviously disconnected. He listened to air, concluding that the whole 'conversation' had been nothing but that. *Hot air!* To say that Matthew Diggerson was angry was like describing Anna as being 'asleep.' But he didn't want to curse, didn't want Anna to hear expletives bouncing around her dreams. Instead, he pictured Busher in unflattering ways, with a big, fat head, for instance, and then with a thick 1970's mustache. Busher wanted to be Burt Reynolds, he thought, and he wished and wished that the little detective, Doyle, were still on the force. Even the Zorn woman would be much more helpful than this new guy. What kind of a name was 'Busher' anyway! Digger thought of murdered colleagues—Tobias Mann, Diana Pell, the adjunct Johna Adams, almost he himself, and now Jolie Matterson—and then pondered statements left unsaid, such as

"We writing teachers are quite susceptible to accidents, aren't we? Being hit by cars, falling down stairs, having our necks throttled and bullets stuck in our temples, knives in our backs!" He considered calling the man back again to say just that, but then the disappointment simply deflated Matthew Diggerson, who pictured Don Quixote's tilting at windmills. "Dulce-Anna" he said to Anna, and then he said it again, singing. The notes sounded broken, unable to fly. When would she wake up?

The released witness photo entered his mind, so he turned on his laptop, accessed the Internet, and found the picture via the region's one daily newspaper. Yes, the car was blue, but was it the blue Elantra from the OVC parking lots? Digger simply couldn't tell, the car was too far away and a little fuzzy, too. Yet it *did* look like that car. What more proof did Busher need to at least begin a murder investigation? At least the stupid man could run that plate, *BB9112!*

Again, Matthew Diggerson closed his eyes, redirected his thoughts away from the OVPD and a mustached dope, and pictured the killer driving away from poor Jolie. From the hallway, a passerby would've thought the scene to be a peaceful one, two sleeping lovers, but the man's thoughts were dark. The killer would want to hide the car, maybe to wash it. How much evidence would stick to the car, to the tires? Unfortunately, quite a bit. Digger felt very sorry for Jolie and a little guilty for not liking her more, for not enjoying her sarcasm as perhaps he could have. He should contact Mary and give her his condolences. Maybe Mary would even join him on his quest to find the killer, to eliminate the bastard. Yes, that's what Digger wanted to do, what he really wanted, to kill the killer, and that realization surprised him just a bit. Mary could be his ally. Her phone number would be Jolie's, and he already had that contact info, right in this laptop. He could call her now, right now!

"Anna," he said instead. "Come back and save me."

On the second day of the Spring Break vacation, the first Sunday, Digger read another OVC email while seated next to Anna, this one about a planned memorial for the Wednesday after the break. It would take place outside the library, weather permitting, and Digger thought of Danny Jones' memorial, of Omar Johns' pontificating, of Don Domberg's striding through the crowed, his shovel beard like a motorboat, leaving people in its wake. That's how he remembered that scene, those two men, and he wondered if Time would repeat the memory this time. Would the administrator give a speech about Jolie? Had he known her well enough? That didn't seem to matter to Omar Johns, who could no doubt make something up that sounded good, like any effective salesman. Would Don come striding over from Tutorial Services, like an old-fashioned steam train with his cattle-knocking beard? Maybe Digger would be asked to speak, what would he say about Jolie? No, he *could* speak, but Digger didn't want to, didn't know what he'd say, didn't have the words for Jolie Matterson, and that was sad. Lou would speak, he was the Humanities Chairperson, and it was his job, his responsibility. Digger hadn't been the Chair for many years, one of which was lost behind a little silver bullet. Silver or gold? Digger always pictured Eliot Gladstone's bullet as 'silver,' as though the man had considered *him* to be the monster. Probably, Professor Happy Rock had thought just that.

"Anna," he said to his wife, so beautiful. "Wake up and save me from all of life's monsters. Wake up and come to Jolie's memorial." But she didn't.

On the Monday following Spring Break, Digger could not find the blue Elantra in its usual place in the faculty/staff parking lot, nor in any of the others he'd rooted out. On Tuesday, a non-teaching day but still with office-hour responsibilities, he began asking anyone who exited faculty/staff cars or who seemed about to enter them whether they knew who owned a blue Hyundai Elantra. The strangers made faces and said, "No" and sometimes, "Sorry," but rarely anything else, such as, "Why do you ask?" His question seemed to worry and confuse most people, as though he were asking about a faculty or staff member with 'two heads' or 'extra fingers on his right hand.' To him, any question about a blue car must mean that its driver had run over Professor Jolie Matterson, but none of the OVC people seemed to make that connection or to go down that road if they had. Digger's motivation was far more 'Anna' than 'Jolie,' whom he'd never felt close to and who'd always pushed him away more than attracted him. He mourned her mainly just as a fellow human being, one who shared the experience of teaching writing and being on tiresome committees and waiting through office hours, helping advisees, all the same responsibilities that Digger had once thought would draw colleagues to his books, which he kept forgetting to bring in for the display case. When he saw the empty shelves, he thought about Jolie's plan to write or perhaps just her sarcasm. He decided that he'd miss that attitude, which brightened the Humanities hallway, gave it a sheen, anyway.

Straight through Spring Break week and into this first week of the semester's second half, March had been cold, rainy, and gloomy, less a lion's growl than a grumble, but winter had still refused to be dragged away by Time, the de-fanger of all beasts, the transformer of lions into lambs. Digger began to think of those dark days as the cause of Anna's continued 'coma' (he tried not to think of that word), as the only impediment to her awakening. With spring's rebirth, he expected her current state to change (and the professor would be correct in that assumption, as only Time would tell). For now, though, both winter and its dreams in Anna held sway.

On Wednesday, the morning of Jolie's memorial (weather permitting), Digger thought with renewed hope of 'Mary,' of how to approach her and convert the unknown woman into his sleuthing cause. A sleuth for the truth. The memorial was scheduled for 4:00, and Digger had emailed his classes that morning about the cancelation of his four-to-five office hour. If any students had had Professor Matterson, Digger wrote that he hoped they could join the memorial, too. He hoped, too, that the rain would hold off, and as he took the very short trip from the FOB to the Classroom Building, so far it had.

In his two afternoon WTNG 200 classes, he was doing the same collaborative 'reasoning review' exercise that he had used in his earlier EN 102's since both courses were at the same spot in the Project Four process, planning and writing. For each of the paired classes, he provided a point and a quotation, and then groups of students (he often used trios) had to add corresponding sentences of explanation, which they'd then add to the board for analysis and potential free minutes—two for 'great' reasoning, one for 'good' explanations. As usual, he stressed that any examples below 'good' earned no minutes but offered everyone valuable illustrations. The 102 students were explaining fictional elements, such as symbolism and personification, while the 200 ones focused on business-oriented problems involving a fictional employee—e.g., ethical issues, performance troubles, etc. The lesson required quick analyses on his part, but Digger had to admit that today he'd been a bit slow, had awarded too many minutes, perhaps, out of sheer mental apathy, for his mind was on a blue Elantra and on Mary, not to mention Anna, always on Anna. And Snodo arose quite often, too, for how could he ever forget a companion so full of life? Jolie appeared as well.

After his 3:00 students had departed, Digger made the short walk to the Main Library, which was skirted by a small crowd. He scanned for familiar faces and for one stranger, for a woman who looked like a 'Mary.' The writing faculty appeared in two small groups, full and part-time, and seeing the small numbers, Digger realized that his department needed to hire at least two new full-time teachers. In the past several years, they'd lost three full-timers—Diana (to murder), Eliot Gladstone (to suicide), and Mary (to retirement, thank goodness)—and now Jolie, and they'd replaced not a single one! The administrators must have been wringing their hands in glee at all the money saved, and Digger thought of Mr. Potter from *It's a Wonderful Life*. Was it wonderful? Digger pulled his thoughts back to the gathering. Of the adjuncts, only three appeared—Dave Jepson, Liz Lawson, and Jay Moore, a tripod of desire, Digger concluded, for each would no doubt be imagining a full-time opening now. That sudden truth, that door opening, surprised him. Was he being unjust? Did any of the three even have a PhD, a requirement for full-time teaching at a four-year college? Digger thought that Dave did, that Liz might have, and that Jay did not. He thought of Jay Moore, the Blinker, as a converted real-estate agent who'd gone to night school to earn his Master's; in fact, Moore had told him that very tale. Could a person earn a Doctorate from a night school or from an online college?

"Who cares!" Digger decided, and then "Nothing matters, and everything matters," one of his mantras. Thinking of Anna and glancing toward the podium for someone who looked like 'Mary,' Digger stopped at the cluster of adjuncts. If the three had formed a rock band, they could have been called 'Cluster of Adjuncts,' maybe punk rock or what some students called "Indie" music, which Digger didn't quite understand. He kept these tangential ideas to himself. The four humans nodded, exchanged brief grimacing smiles, offered hopes that the clouds wouldn't give way, and expressed their continuing shock about Jolie.

"Where are the two new people?" said Digger. "Ben, whose last name I can't remember, and Liz George, whose name I can't forget."

"Oh, I love Elizabeth George!" said Liz, adding "the writer" and then "but don't call our Elizabeth 'Liz.' She won't let even *me* do that, one Liz to another."

"She *is* a little prickly," said Dave.

"Sort of like Jolie was," said Jay, who then blinked and added, "Such a horrible accident."

"Bodine," said Dave oddly, and although he started to explain that strange utterance, Digger cut in. He couldn't help himself, for that word, 'accident,' had become a trigger, not to mention that Moore by his own admission owned a Hyundai, the murder weapon, in Digger's mind.

"It was no 'accident'!" he declared, causing the three adjuncts to widen their eyes, frown, and create fragmented exclamations of "What" and "Why."

"Remember my wife, Anna," Digger stated, not asking a question. "She was hit, too, and by a *blue* car, too, but she lived. The cops said 'accident' then, too, and they said 'drunk driver.' *Drunk driver?* Jolie was run down in the late afternoon, not exactly the deadliest time for drunk drivers, is it? And don't forget about the vandalized gravestones from last summer. Tobias', Diana's, and more. Something's going on here, and I should know because I've been stalked before. More than once, by more than one sicko, too, and I can feel it again. Murder!"

If Digger's blood hadn't been boiling, if Anna were not still lying unconscious in a nursing home, and if he were not attending the memorial for a colleague crushed by a car, he might have laughed out loud at the three speechless faces around him, two with wide eyes and one blinking like an owl. "Of course, I might be wrong," he said and left the group. He imagined an explosion of chattering but didn't really care. Let them gossip. Mad Matthew Diggerson! Maybe even another full-time opening! Well, if nobody else could see the truth, that it was all happening again, Murder U but with a different MO this time—from knives, to hands, to revolvers, to a blue Hyundai Elantra—then who cared if Diggerson appeared to have lost his wits? *Far better to lose those than your life—or your wife.* Besides, how paranoid could a person with a bullet lodged in his head be?

Making his way around several other people clusters, Digger decompressed and nodded hello to teachers he somewhat knew and even to ones he didn't, and then his own tribe of full-timers greeted him: Lou, Todd, Jeff, Don Domberg, and even the recently retired Mary. Not the 'Mary' he wanted to see, but Digger smiled and said hello to her first, shook hands, inquired about retirement and its treatment. He thought of advising the whole group to retire while they still could, but a second mad soliloquy just wasn't in him at the moment. Who knew, too—maybe the killer was standing right in this cluster, or in an adjoining one, maybe in that rock group, Cluster of Adjuncts. It suddenly struck him that the vandalism and then Anna's being targeted, those two events, might have been red herrings, a set up to hide the real goal: getting rid of Jolie and opening up a new full-time position. *Realistic?* Digger decided to brainstorm this new angle later, but he berated himself for not at least entertaining it during those long winter months. What other possibilities had blinders prevented him from seeing? *Good fences* might make *good neighbors*, but they blocked objectivity, too.

"Robert Frost," said Digger, and then he almost giggled at the absurdity of the thought's having escaped unbidden.

"What?" said Lou.

"Frost?" said Todd.

"Ha, ha!" said Don.

Jeff said nothing.

"I was just thinking of Robert Frost," said Digger, just a bit sheepishly, but before he could explain, metal screeched, squeaked, and shrieked, making the crowd duck a bit, perhaps thinking of attacking seagulls. Omar Johns was fumbling at the podium with the microphone.

"You'd think that an *administrator* would know how to use a microphone," said Don Domberg sarcastically.

After wrestling with the mic for a few more seconds, Omar shrugged sheepishly and then gave a short speech that was more about the OVC 'family' than 'Jolie' specifically, but he did mention her full name a few times. Then one of Jolie's past students read a poem he'd apparently written about being different and choosing his own path, halfway through which Don leaned toward Digger and said, "The road not taken, eh?" Digger responded with that quick, bunched-lip smile popular at funerals, and then somebody else spoke, another man. Digger thought that Jolie would have raged about 'all these men speakers' at her eulogy, but mainly he was waiting for a woman to take the 'stage,' for Jolie's partner in life, the left-behind Mary. But the memorial ended with the man's request for a minute of silence in Jolie Matterson's memory. Everybody bowed his or her head, Digger's realizing that Lou would not be speaking. The 'minute' ended early. "Where have all the Marys gone?" Digger thought in song, and then he noticed all the clusters breaking up, their individual parts moving off. That image reminded Digger of something, a picture that would not quite focus.

The others must have said 'goodbye,' but Digger hadn't really heard any voices. Soon, he was standing alone, the center of an expanding circle, and the writing teacher pictured the Big Bang, the birth and flight of the universe. *Am I the center of all this?* he thought, *Or is Tobias? Is Jolie? Definitely not Anna. Where did this story begin? Where would it end?*

At that point, a figure, a somewhat familiar man, approached him and stopped, his right hand held out. Digger took it. "Ben Bodine," said the man, who then looked about at the now empty quad. "What did I miss?"

CHAPTER NINE

THE ESSAY CHARACTERISTICS OUTCOME

The typical college essay offers an introduction, a series of supporting paragraphs (the 'body'), and a conclusion, but this document looks far different than the usual five-paragraph high school paper. College essays contain more information and tactics, such as more varied planning in body paragraphs (perhaps a compare-contrast structure instead of the simpler illustration one), more audience awareness (e.g., extensive reasoning), a more narrowed choice of topics (no reports on the 'universe,' for instance), more research (from better sources, like databases)—just plain 'more.' Essays need logical organizations, clear focusing points, specific development, and they should be delivered by grammatically competent writers, too.

The hauntings were over, at least during the day. The blood fountain now seemed almost pretty in his mind, and he was glad that the bitchy woman, the disrespectful witch, was gone, erased, and this incident would keep the nest buzzing, careening about in all directions. Still, her *cleaning* had caused some trouble, some effort, since a witness had seen a blue car and had taken a fuzzy picture of it, one shown on the news repeatedly, a blue blur in the distance. His plate number could not be seen, though, and no cops had shown up at his door, not this time, since his connection to the victim was tenuous. Still, the Elantra was 'hot,' the piece of crap. Therefore, he had covered it with a tarp and planned to tell his neighbors that it wouldn't run, had stopped finally. Nobody asked. The 'new' car had cost close to two grand, and it was older than his Elantra, for God's sake. A black Toyota Corolla, ran well. No dents, no hubcaps, either. And it was black, with slightly tinted glass, too. A nice touch of 'bad boy' for his new wheels. With the Hyundai, that faithful piece of junk (if it were an old horse, set out to pasture, he would have called it 'Blue'), he'd done a proper cleaning. Now he could do more, but what was left?

His father was checked off, sputtered away like a landed clam, gulping away helplessly, and that was the big erasure, the capital 'E.' His mother, she was still around, in a way, during the darkest hours of night, but even her voice was disappearing, her 'not enough' whispers. And his sister, she could be avoided, living so far away. In fact, Bevy was clearly avoiding them all, not even deeming funerals worth her attendance. *Good!* She'd escaped in her own fashion, but why hadn't he gone that simple route? Attachments to his mother, and also what repels can attract. Too damn easy to run, too, and too much stuff to do. That sounded almost poetic, and he smiled as he worked. *Stuff to do*, he thought. Past wrongs to right, age spots to erase. What had his mother called that stuff, that cosmetic to cover skin trouble, old age blemishes? *Vanisher!* It was light brown, and his mother had dabbed it all over her cheeks, chin, and neck, even more so as her old face grew more witchlike. Her sickness. Then he smiled. That's who he could be—The Vanisher! It sounded just like a silly superhero, and he laughed quietly as he worked. Maybe Bevy needed his attention, especially if she caused any trouble with the will.

A passerby might have seen the smiling worker and thought him to be either quite content in life or possibly diminished in mental capabilities. Neither case would have been true.

March's rain stretched into April, the only difference being a handful of degrees in temperature. Digger searched for the blue Elantra every day, but it was *gone*. How suspicious was that! After school and around his trips to Breezy Seas, Digger once again canvassed garages and now used-car lots, scanning for blue Elantras with dents. Then he made pit stops at home, he wanted to be at Breezy Seas, and when there, he dreamed of being at home with Anna. Bumper forgave his absences. His mother forgave his lack of visits. "You stay with Anna!" she'd admonished him by phone, as though it were her idea, and the son gave his mother that small power.

The house was so quiet. Even the bay muffled its endless movements, the white, frothy spray above, the dark, coiling currents below. He could look out his back window and see forsythia now, growing yellow and wild, untamed, in Graham's yard. His absent neighbors. *Where the hell was Donna?* Digger hadn't seen Graham's wife in a long time—when? *Last summer maybe.* He looked back into his own unruly yard and saw Bumper staring at him from outside the rickety gate. Digger waved. Bumper was silent, too, had always been the quietest of cats. Except for his purring, a motorboat at sea yet racing for shore. The yard seemed like a picture, almost motionless, and suddenly Digger's mind shifted in time, bringing the image of two little cats, black and white both, seated like bowling pins near the porch and staring up at him as he looked out the door. *Shyla and Skittles.* A lifetime ago and only yesterday, both at the same time. *One of Time's tricks,* thought Digger. To make a person think that no years were passing and then to strike, to rip something away. Snodo, Simba, two little feral cats. Parents, siblings, friends. Anna? How could she still be asleep? Four months now, yet he himself had survived for much longer, more than three times that length. Anna's vitals were *good*, her brain was functioning. She just wasn't ready yet to rejoin the world. Who could blame her?

However, the cottage was *nothing*, not a home, not a harbor, without Anna's presence. To breathe, it needed Anna's golden aura, and Digger had spent as little time as possible at 'home.' Breezy Seas seemed more like home than this small structure, this location, yet still Digger was drawn to the view out his back windows. How much of his life had been spent *right here*, trying to make sense of it all, trying to steady his footing on the shifting ground? Wobbling again, and maybe that was the moral, the truth, that the ground never stopped shifting. That smooth sailing was just an illusion, something humanity dreamed up to stave off insanity. Dogs and cats did that, too, kept the madness at bay.

Digger opened the back door and called to Bumper, who jumped the gate and trotted across the yard.

"Just like a dog," Digger heard and then found half of Graham's head over the fence dividing the two properties. Digger waved to Graham, bent and petted Bumper, and then walked down his steps to talk with his neighbor.

Approaching, he could still see just the upper half of the man's head, and suddenly the image seemed deceptive: a man showing only half his thoughts. Why had he never added 'Graham' to his suspects list, for the fellow lived right beside him? And where was Donna? Had he buried her out back one dark night, perhaps next to the rat?

"How's your wife?" the neighbor's head said, but Digger could see just his eyes. "Has she woken up yet?"

"No, but her vitals are good, and her mind's working fine. She's just healing up."

"Good, good," said Graham, and then "Wild, that's wild." It sounded like a catch phrase, outdated, though, something from the 1960's or 70's. Digger thought of Detective Busher's mustache and then of the silly word "Groovy," but his mind was dark. His neighbor's forehead was nodding, showed a handful of horizontal lines, dipped in the center, and Digger thought of the 'V' that formed above Anna's beautiful eyes when she was troubled or lost in thought. "That's good," Graham said again.

"How's Donna?" said Digger to the nodding head. "I haven't seen her in months." *Where's her body?* With the rat?

Graham stopped nodding. "She's been at her mother's house, a lot. Her mother broke her hip, so she's been taking care of both her mother and father. I've been left to do the cooking. Can you cook, Digger?"

Had that been a question or a plea? Did Graham actually want him to provide a hot meal? To Digger, Graham no longer looked suspicious, just helpless, a little pathetic even with his fence-divided face angled down, all those lines on his forehead. Digger thought of Forrest Gump at the end of that epic movie. Forrest Gump on his bench when the feather that had danced about the sky and then landed near the seated man at the film's beginning flew off again at the end as the sweet music began to play. Digger tried to remember that melody, but the notes wouldn't form. Nothing but the wind now whispered, soft yet insistent as always along the bay.

"Just salmon," said Digger, adding, "Try that, try salmon; you can't ruin it because it's so fatty, the good kind, healthy. You can't overcook salmon."

"It's hard to be without our women," said Graham, and behind him the many tentacled forsythia wriggled in the faint breezes like something demented, something in great pain. *Our women.* Digger thought of Anna and then of the faceless 'Mary,' of Jolie Matterson.

Graham sauntered off soon after making his 'hard' conclusion, just another man missing his woman. Back inside his kitchen, Digger felt Bumper running figure eights around his legs, reminding him of feeding time or arguing for one, anyway. "You want second breakfast?" Digger said into those big golden eyes, which communicated "Yes" and more emotions, too, so Digger poured a little more kibble into the cat's bowl. Maybe he'd take Bumper to visit Anna today. Certainly, Breezy Seas could relax its no-pet policy on a Friday. No, he had to go to OVC first, so he wouldn't return here until much later. And he couldn't keep track of Bumper down Ward C, anyway, since the cat would no doubt venture off on his own and get lost. Being as mysterious as he was, Bumper would probably be like that nursing home psychic feline who labeled the soon-to-be-dead by jumping up on their beds and waiting with them. Waiting for death. *Don't go there!* Don't take the path ending in the *black river*, its thick waters. Digger thought instead of that prophetic feline, a tiger cat in his memories. Where had that cat story taken place and when? Ten years ago? Everything was always a decade past. No, Digger wouldn't bring Bumper today. Maybe tomorrow.

He sat at the table, heard Bumper crunching the kibble, and realized that he had to eat something, too. All he ever seemed to eat was eggs. He was turning into a damn lizard. Yes, getting harder on the outside. Armored scales. Was this his future? A life alone and all this space. How could he possibly fill the space? Would he write more mysteries? Billy D seemed played out, but what about another series? Maybe he could have an adjunct hero this time, lots of conflict with full-timers there and even with other part-timers, all of whom would want the favor of the Chair, and full-time work. That possibility caused Digger to shift in his chair. *No!* Could that very scenario be playing out now? Jolie's empty position right now, Mary's for the past year, and more. The full-time Humanities faculty list was 'growing thin,' he concluded again, thinking of Elrond and *Lord of the Rings*. He had to eat. Too many thoughts bouncing around in his empty body. He needed his notebook to capture them, yet he stayed seated, the cat's crunching away at his feet.

Digger pulled his mind back to a new mystery series, an adjunct protagonist, someone named 'Dan.' He'd always liked the name 'Dan' and even 'Daniel.' The guy's mother would call him 'Daniel,' but everyone else just 'Dan' or maybe a nickname. Just like his own mother and 'Matthew.' "The acronym 'WHAT,'" thought Digger. *Write How it Actually Transpired.* He started to invent titles, kitschy ones like "Write to the Heart," "All the Write Moves," "Write to Die."

Silly. He had to eat. He no longer felt up to creating a new world in order to make up for the present one. Digger went to the fridge to get a couple eggs.

On the way to Ocean View College, the writing teacher thought about creating a new course, Mystery 200, and wondered how the administration would feel about that. Omar Johns would worry about supply/demand and about paying someone else to make up for Digger's teaching a low-enrollment Mystery Writing one. As he kept an eye out for blue Elantras, Digger wondered where all these creative thoughts were coming from and why. Was it a sign that Anna was awakening, both her life and his own, or was he unconsciously preparing for a life without her?

At school, as he got out of his Yaris, Digger saw the adjunct Jay Moore drive by—in a reddish car, *maroon*—and Moore turned his wide head at Digger and blinked in passing. The adjunct must be feeling lucky if he thought he could find a parking spot this close at this time of day. Digger waved and noted that the car was in fact an Elantra, stamped with that name on the back. Could Jay have traded in a blue model or even had this one painted? Digger watched the car disappear, no spaces being available here.

In his office before the 11:00 class, Digger admitted that Jay's maroon car looked like it needed new paint, so he released the man from his suspects list—or at least put a light slash through his name on the brainstorming visuals, adding 'wrong car—maroon' near the adjunct's name. Once again, he wondered about the part-timers, about reasons to kill, and decided that prestige was a strong motivation, for going from part- to full-time brought more than just money. However, if the adjuncts knew about all the extra work, Digger thought—the committees and advisees and extra hours—then they might not be so *gung-ho* about the switch. Dave, Liz, Elizabeth, and Ben. To his brainstorming, the mind map, he added their names with lines from Jolie's, and then he created lines to the words 'prestige,' 'money,' 'life goal.' All motivators. But incentive enough to kill? What did Anna have to do with any of those words? *Red herring,* thought the rhetorically minded composition professor. *False trail?* He added those words to a line ending with 'Anna.' Where all lines ended. Always.

As he worked on his notes, Matthew Diggerson thought of beginnings, middles, and endings. The vandalism, Anna, Jolie, and what else? Was the cemetery the beginning? Was Jolie the ending? What was the 'body,' anyway? What was Digger missing? He was missing Anna.

A couple hours later, after two classes, he heard Lou coming down the hall, his long strides, and then the box-headed thin man appeared in his doorway. "Did you finally bring your books?" he said. "Gloria keeps complaining about that empty display case."

Digger smiled. He had remembered and put the books in his briefcase that very morning so that he wouldn't yet again forget. The display case didn't seem to matter much these days, but why not a ray of sunshine? He lifted the four books in a little pile, got up, and handed them to the Humanities Chair, who took them solemnly and said, "And now we will celebrate some writing. And like the Dream Board, maybe that display case will spur us all to *do* what we love to teach."

Digger almost laughed. Lou's words were true but sounded overly formal, especially when the books he carried announced names like *Perilous Persuasion.*

"By the way, my friend," said Lou, "did I tell you that your journal, that editor, contacted me about my peer-review article? I should find out within a few weeks whether or not they want to publish it."

"That's great, Lou, but don't count the weeks. 'A few' will turn into five or six weeks fast. It's a slow, slow process, especially when the pair of reviewers gets involved."

"I look forward to it. My angle's not the usual one, you know. As we've mentioned before, most students don't like peer reviews."

"You'll be tilting at windmills, Lou, and that's always sort of fun."

"Don Quixote, good. I'll have Angela call me 'Don' from now on."

"Wait until the article's accepted, and maybe until the reviewers have ripped it apart. I've never revised anything like I did those scholarly articles. First, they want *more proof,* more explaining, but next they want *fewer words.* Then when you return the draft, you don't hear from them for a month, or more. Don't hold your breath *ever.*"

"Yeah, that's all we need around here, another full-time opening. I've already talked with Omar about getting a couple new full-timers."

Our ranks are getting *thin,*" said Digger, but the other man failed to catch his Tolkien reference.

"I suggested two openings, one in-house, one out. That way we get some new blood, but we also keep the adjuncts interested, keep the carrot extended."

"The possibility of advancement," said Digger. "I remember that nice feeling." Digger thought of voicing his suspicions about Jolie's 'accident,' but he kept them to himself. He'd never talked to colleagues about his suspicions, mainly because most had involved them.

"Let me get these beauties into the box!" said Lou, and then Digger's doorway was empty. He thought that he heard loping footsteps attenuating. He thought of his books in the case and felt good for a change. Then his mind shifted as it did so often these days, weeks, months. He thought of Eliot Gladstone standing before the display case and looking down at the four books. *Eliot.* Envy and bitterness, what a brew! Did anyone else down this hallway sip from the same cauldron? And in that instant, Digger knew, came to that obvious conclusion a person has right before realizing that he or she is wrong: *An adjunct did it!* Knocked off Jolie to create one too many openings, and what of Anna? An innocent bystander, a *red herring*. Who but a composition teacher would know about fallacies in logic, about laying false trails. *False trails!* He'd thought of that before, and that squiggly line made much more sense now.

But which adjunct?

One blinked like mad (Jay Moore), another mandated a formal salutation (Elizabeth George), and then there was the new Ben guy, whose last name wouldn't stay in Digger's mind, sounded like a cow. *Bovine.* Ben *Bodine!* After Jolie's memorial the previous month, when Digger had told the man what he'd 'missed,' the new adjunct had said "Who's Jolie?" Had he been acting, or could he have been that clueless?

Ben had seemed genuine, and hadn't Digger already slashed Jay Moore off his list? Jay didn't even have a PhD, for that matter, so he couldn't be in line for any in-house opening. Did Ben or Elizabeth George? He couldn't see a woman behind the wheel, either, but why not? A woman driver would add another layer of motivation, too, more possible envy. Anna was certainly beautiful, but Jolie? Not exactly attractive in the usual way, but who knows? Anybody who'd steer a car into a human being wasn't exactly *normal*.

Digger suddenly remembered his 2:00 class and looked out the narrow window at the clock towers. Time to go. The hallway was empty, but Digger found one of his suspects standing before the display case, which now held not only his own four books, propped up on the top right and taking up half the shelf, but two of Diana Pell's tomes of poetry, including her final one, *Seasonings*. Digger was glad to see her books, too.

Ben Bovine (*Bodine!*) said, "Who's Diana Pell? Is she full-time?"

Digger decided to see how the man would react to the word 'murder.' "Diana was a long-time full-timer, even once the state's Poet Laureate, but she was *murdered* several years back, killed by another faculty member."

"No kidding," said the adjunct. "Lou didn't include *that* history in his welcoming brochure." He smiled at his own wording.

Digger tried again. "Our hallway's had a colorful past. Another member was *murdered* a couple decades back, along with the janitor."

The news made no dent in Ben Bodine's demeanor, and then the implacable adjunct explained why. "I graduated from OVC, so I know all about the history. I was just joking about Lou's not telling me. I had Lou as a teacher, but not you and not Professor Mann, the one who died. One of the ones. I might have had that Gladstone guy for Professional Writing, hard to remember."

"You wouldn't have forgotten Eliot," said Digger, adding, "Or Tobias, or even Dan Pinsky, the janitor who was killed. He was a memorable fellow!"

"What about the current janitor?" said Bodine. "He's quite the colorful chap, with those big headphones. Maybe he's the killer this time. Isn't it always the butler or the 'maintenance engineer'?"

For an instant, Digger compared this new adjunct to the old student, George North, since both seemed to share a talent for transitioning topics. "George is all right," said Digger, feeling a need to stand up for his ex-student, not to mention for his own chosen genre, murder mysteries. "He actually went to school here, too."

"And majored in Janitorial Services! I didn't know OVC had that subject." Ben Bodine laughed at his own joke, and Digger thought of Jolie. They would have enjoyed each other. Then he felt a little guilty for that comparison.

"I should have majored in that field; I'd be much richer," said the adjunct, who had curly hair that looked a bit unnatural. "But I'd go absolutely bonkers if all I did all day was mop and clean, mop and clean, back and forth, you know? All that repetition."

"What about us?" said Digger, still wanting to stand up for George North. "What about all *our* repetition? The constant notes to students to go further with their explanations, to listen for commas and comma splices, to 'show' instead of just 'telling.' All jobs have repetition, and they have to, so that the job doers get really good at their craft."

"Good with a *mop*?" said Curly, and Digger deflected the sarcastic question and thought instead of his upcoming class. He didn't want *this* conversation to make him late.

"I've got to go, Ben. Two o'clock class. You keep on writing so that you can add something to this case."

As he started down the stairs, Digger felt a little small about his parting shot at a colleague, but then when he heard a final statement cast his way, "What we all need is to inherit millions," the small guilt trickled away. On the short walk connecting the Faculty Office Building to the one with classrooms, Digger watched two seagulls swish through the blue sky and wondered about inheritances. He never considered one, probably because his father had died so long ago. While his mother never seemed to lack for money, she'd no doubt need the house to finance her extreme old age. Was that stage already here? The son could not picture his mother in a nursing home, a place like Breezy Seas. Above, the pair of gulls was riding the breeze, swooping, looping, looking like a pair of fighter planes, a dog fight. How many people dreamed of inheriting a fortune? How many would be disappointed? Seemingly in answer, one of the distant seagulls screamed, and a startled Matthew Diggerson grinned.

Two hours later, two more classes completed, Digger smiled again upon climbing the stairs and seeing the display case and his four books: *Composition Murder, Murderous Mistakes, Perilous Persuasion, and Ominous Organization.* The colors green and cobalt blue, gold and red—pretty. Billy D's dogs, too, the fictional Simba and Snodo. Seeing the books made Digger want to create another, but that would have to wait. Diana's two displayed books were both golden brown, and looking at them, he pictured the stoic yet classy woman, her slow, reluctant smile, like sunshine bursting at last through an overcast sky. He smiled in her honor. Had she even read his books? Not the third and fourth, which were created after Eliot killed her, but what about the first two? Digger couldn't remember, and he thought that was a good thing. If he'd harbored resentment towards his colleague, it was gone now. Maybe Time wasn't always an adversary.

The vestibule was empty, had been all day. Where was Gloria? He thought of how George had called the secretary "the Hair" and wondered where she was. Gloria had read all four of his books, the only OVC person to have shown such interest. Gloria, Anna, and his mother—those were his three real fans. He hoped that Gloria wasn't sick.

He walked alone to his office to wait for 5:00, which came slowly but surely. At five o'clock, the clock tower's twin reaching shadows looked stubbier each lengthening day as spring progressed, pushing back the night. As usual, upon leaving, Digger saw George North, and he thought of Ben Bodine's summation about 'back and forth, over and over.' That's what he hated about gossip, the way it added unwanted images whenever the object of the rumor appeared. Digger had to admit that George's headphones were larger than most; they would probably drown out a jackhammer. To say hello and goodbye to the man, Digger had to tap him on the shoulder, and when George slipped off his headphones, Digger got a surprise. The chorus to "Billy, Don't Be a Hero" poured from the set. George would definitely go deaf if he weren't more careful.

"What's that song, George?"

"It's one of yours, professor." George smiled. When didn't he? "I heard you mumbling it last semester some time, so I Googled the 'Billy' part and then YouTubed it. Since then it's been stuck in my head."

"I know what you mean. I woke up with that melody in mind for about two straight weeks."

"It was written by some band from the 70's, Paper Lace, who dressed up in soldier outfits. The rest of their stuff was just pop shlop, but this one's a classic. As old as you are, eh, Professor!"

Digger left soon after that, hearing George's singing as he descended the stairs: "Billy, don't be a hero, come back to me. Don't be a fool with your life." George was pretty far out of tune and didn't have the lyrics quite right, either, but singing was a good thing. He thought of Anna, then he wondered whom George was picturing. Was he singing to anyone in particular? Digger hoped so.

Along the roadways, the forsythia glowed, and all the maple trees were growing fat red fingers, soon to burst. In all this rebirth, Anna was surely to waken.

At Breezy Seas, Digger noticed the orange flowers—what were they called? Snap dragons? Somebody had planted bulbs. The front-desk person was missing, and Digger again thought of Gloria Swanson and wondered where she'd been lately and why. Ward C looked deserted, too. Maybe everyone was eating? But shouldn't somebody be here? Hadn't one of the patients died strangely last fall, under some peculiar circumstances? Digger expected to see somebody, and he felt a little ticked off that he didn't. *Security, please!* Into each doorway, he glanced in at the slumbering old men and women, mostly women. Wives whose husbands had passed long ago. He could hear his own footsteps clumping down the hallway.

When he entered Anna's room, he saw that her eyes looked more green than blue today and connected the color to the sun coming through all the windows from the opposite rooms. Then he thought, "Eyes!" Then he stood and gawked. Then he saw a small smile form on his wife's face, and then he went to pieces, crying and saying "Anna!" and crying, over and over.

He was touching her face and getting her wet, and then other people were in the room, too, a couple of them. He heard "O-oh-o!" and knew who that was, and then he heard, "Get the doctor, Ana!" and knew who that was, too. "I told you, Professor!" said Nurse Addie. "I told you that her vitals were good! Oh, she's a fighter is Anna!"

And Digger just wept and said, "Anna, Anna!" and cried some more and said to Nurse Addie, "Call me 'Digger,' remember?" and then the tears just ended. He had simply run out of water, and he thought of those late summer monsoons in Tucson, Arizona, during his graduate school days, how the rains would shut off abruptly, the same time each late afternoon, just like a faucet. That's how his weeping stopped.

Anna was so weak, but still his wife smiled. He bent and kissed her, and Nurse Addie said, "Digger, let her breathe!" but not unkindly.

Anna said, "You look so young, Matt. How can you look so young?"

Digger heard Bob Dylan singing, that wonderful gravely rawness—"I was so much older then, I'm younger than that now"—and finally he understood those words. A person *could* get younger, even as Time tore away his days.

CHAPTER TEN

THE SELF-REFLECTION
OUTCOME

The 'daddy' of all outcomes, awareness is a writer's ultimate goal
—i.e., an unbiased self-reflection about his or her skills and
processes. Students need to recognize their inconsistencies and to
revise and/or edit for them. Are they prone to making broad
explanatory statements? Do they rely on weak verbs? Did they
rush the ideas-generating step? Habits being the enemy of growth,
the obstacle to change, students must be taught to see problematic
patterns, to understand the issues, both how to spot and then fix the
inconsistencies carried from one paper to the next. Objectivity is
king—for both writers and humans in general!

Silence, darkness, red numbers. Every night was the same, the
only difference being the numbers. Time's red slashes. Who
was it who'd focused on Time, got him to thinking about it
long ago, back when he 'wore a younger man's clothes,' as that
singer said, *Billy Joel*? Back when he was too friggin' young to
really know or recognize the fleeting nature of days! Yeah, it
was Diggerson, in response to some reading, probably to that
one about slaughterhouses he said he always used. Diggerson,
in one of his pensive, philosophical moments, not so much
about how wonderful writing was, or could be, but about life
itself, as though he'd discovered all of its secrets, had
possessed all of its keys. Time? Time, he'd said, something

about being old enough to realize that man's only enemy was Time. He hadn't even been that old at the time, younger than most of the OVC walking dead. Ocean View College. Curse or salvation? Maybe both.

Why did Diggerson have to be erased? Let alone his wife, but she'd been a distraction. A false path from the real targets. The Jolie bitch had been too mean, his own father too friggin' everything, and Diggerson, well, he was just *too damn nice!* Both extremes—bitchy and nice—led to the same damn bitterness, the itch that just couldn't be scratched. Not in any other way, anyway. Just *erasure!* Cleaning up the stains, which were always caused by people.

What had that *blowhard* Professor Mann said, or rather quoted since he himself had never said anything worth quoting? No, not Mann, but he'd quoted a poet or some old philosophical guy. 'Men lead quiet lives of desperation.' Something like that, anyway, 'leading lives' and 'desperation,' definitely. Back then, the quote had made no impression on anyone, just another sound bite from another arrogant old man, but now? Yes, he had to admit to a life led in some *desperation*, to a life wasted even. Wrong paths, dead ends. But that was the point in all of this, right? The whacking of the tombs and then just the whacking, to forge a new path, to break through barriers. To close doors. To lock away the corpses. When the *will* came through, then *life* could begin again.

Anna had lost only a dozen pounds and had joked that everybody should have let her sleep until at least fifteen pounds had burned away, and unlike Digger, after her 'coma,' Anna remembered everything, even the chocolates. "What happened to the box of chocolates?" she'd asked, clearly concerned.

Digger said that the Candy Man had replaced them, that they'd been delicious, especially the jellies, that he'd eaten one every day and thanked her each time. Anna had been glad, but she asked repeatedly about her fall students. What about the final projects in her Design class? What about the Art History final exams? Digger didn't know since nobody had ever contacted him about those classes. Probably the Art Department Chairperson had used her materials on Bridges to finish her classes for her, or maybe the projects and exams had just been canceled due to the circumstances. That 'V' had appeared on Anna's forehead, but the intersecting lines looked a little thinner than before. Perhaps due to her weight loss. Thin already, she'd had little weight to spare, but her spirits were high, right from that first waking moment.

One early May afternoon, Anna declared that she wanted French fries for lunch, and Nurse Addie said, "Then French fries you shall have, got to get some fat on you, Anna Diggerson!"

"French fries?" said Digger, laughing. "I don't remember getting any French fries. All you folks ever gave me was fish and spinach!"

"You were a more difficult patient, Digger," said the hefty nurse, but all three people knew that she was joking. As she left, Digger and Anna saw the aide Ana Cepatos pass by, following a mop. She looked in at them with her big eyes and little mouth. She looked happy. "O-Oh-o!" called Digger, giggling, and they heard the young woman's soft laughter.

"If I were to paint her laughter, I would use petals," said Anna.

"Rose petals," said Digger.

"White rose petals, young ones."

Alone, together, the couple painted in the sky.

Problems. Dark images. Messes! He couldn't get to them at Breezy Seas, and the cracker-angle was now gone. Everybody knew about Diggerson's wife, how she'd woken up all happy and ready to go, but was she still there, at Breezy Seas? Easy enough to find out, just call the place, say he was one of Diggerson's teaching friends, and enquire about 'Anna,' that was her name. All innocent enough. Then he could mention a 'surprise' he was planning—that was certainly true!—and request the date of her return home, perhaps the time, too, yes, that would be most helpful, thank you very much.

Diggerson had been a patient there, too, long ago. Too bad they couldn't stay at the nursing home and haunt the place, along with his father. Too bad he couldn't jam crackers down their throats. He'd have to run them over again, risk another red fountain. No, don't think of that geyser. Just remember the cleaning, the good and the bad, to balance things, not that Diggerson had been particularly 'good,' but he hadn't been 'bad' like his father or the Jolie bitch. People as pieces, obstacles. Just like chess, which his mother had taught him long ago, always letting him be 'white,' giving her little son the first move. The Jolie bitch would've been a bishop, lordly, always moving away, sideward. His father, even absent, was the King, black, but was his mother the Queen? She didn't quite fit that role, his *not-enough* mother. Yes, she was the Queen, but more like the weeping Madonna than a dark Disney queen. What was Diggerson? A knight, definitely, and his wife? Just a pawn. Game, set, and match, and then the estate money would come rolling in and he could roll elsewhere, anywhere, begin again, the slate clean. But how to finish? Where to strike? At that nice little house? At OVC?

No, at Breezy Seas, that's the place. Two birds with one stone. He'd wait out back, away from any cameras, and when they came out, all happy with dreams of 'home,' then vroom, vroom presto! *Two little birdies*. From behind, that's how he'd do it, that's what worked. And his new car was quiet, not like that sputtering old clunker! He wondered how much he'd get for the Elantra. Still ran, just made noises. And had a *blood* problem, of course. See, he could laugh at the fountain, now.

The spring semester ended close to mid-May, so Digger prepared himself mentally for the onslaught of papers, fifteen to twenty in four classes—seventy some papers total. The mornings of focused work bothered him not at all, though, for Anna would be *released* in just a few days. They would go *home*. Anna would fill the house again, and they would talk about Snodo and look at old photographs of her and Simba. Anna would paint one of the photos, and Digger would hang the work—warm and cool colors—in the living room. Maybe Bumper would allow himself to be walked on the beach. Probably not. Maybe they'd go to the pound and find another canine friend, someone in need. Probably not yet.

On the last day of classes, Digger sat alone in his 4:00 to 5:00 office hour, undoubtedly the most solitudinal time for this odd Humanities hallway except the deep hours of the night because only he inhabited the whole building, only he and perhaps George North down below, working his way up the corridors. No night-course teaching adjuncts would appear this early, probably not until 5:30 for their 6:00 classes, and Gloria was almost always gone by 4:00. This past semester, Digger had rarely seen the motherly secretary, who luckily hadn't been ill, just truant. Digger wanted to skip out early, too. How often had he sat by himself and watched the clock towers' shadows reaching out, longer and longer? Luckily, the FOB was far enough to the side for him to avoid those elongated arms, which could easily be turned into symbols. This semester had gone well, just like the last one. Even the few potential un-coachable students had rounded out pretty well. On her last report, Kaitlyn had even earned the 'A' she so clearly, to herself, deserved. Okay, an 'A-.' Probably, her final paper, a memo to him about her own current writing strengths and weaknesses, would've been submitted already, but Matthew Diggerson didn't feel like grading yet. He just wanted to relax, to watch the towers' shadows, to think of Anna. If she were to paint him, he'd suggest this very scene, alone in the deepening shadows of his office. He pictured the aura of Wyeth's solitary hound in *Master Bedroom*. In Anna's picture, he would be that old, white dog.

He imagined, too, all the directions Nurse Addie would soon give him about taking care of Anna at home, about all the food and the exercises. He remembered the facts well, so he decided to do what he always did, start listing. He got out his notebook, the paper kind that students no longer seemed to own, turned to a clean page and wrote two sub-titles: Food and Exercise. Under Food, he listed 'salmon' first and then kept jotting down all the items recommended to him by Doctor Sam a decade past. Under Exercises, he listed 'walks' and then some of the muscle builders that Nurse Addie had helped him with, making up names like 'Leg Ups' and 'Arm Curls.' He imagined showing Nurse Addie his list just as she was about to harangue him with advice. He imagined laughing at her surprise, at the small theft of her expertise.

The right clock tower tended to run fast, always a few minutes ahead of Time, and Digger thought that might be a nice way to live, just out of Time's reach. But how to get far enough from its fingers? By being *happy*, that was how. Happiness was Time's enemy because that state made the nemesis disappear. And Digger did feel happy, for the shadows had mostly been pushed away when Anna's eyes had opened. Digger rarely thought about a blue Elantra or about job-hungry adjuncts, about villains from the past. In fact, he'd thought of the skeleton for a fifth Billy D Wilder tale, a happy ending involving his previously star-crossed protagonist and one lost love, Lana. *Grave Errors*, that would be its name, and some of the past year's events would form the plot, with 'grammar' chapter titles like 'Run-ons' and 'Fragments.' In his second book, *Murderous Mistakes*, he'd used titles like that, maybe the exact ones, so he'd have to check that text in order to avoid repetitive content. Yet who in the new tale would be the villain? Undetermined, as of yet.

The 'estate' still loomed large in his imagination, big enough to fertilize a future. Big enough to encompass six grocery stores and all those people in them. Six store managers, and he hadn't been *good enough* to manage even one, even that dump in Middleburg surrounded by all those immigrants. Well, he'd soon sell them all, and then who knows what would happen to those cushy jobs? When the will cleared probate, then he'd get his due—unless Bev, little Bevy, prolonged the process by contesting it. Maybe she would, maybe she'd get nothing, how would he know? Daddy always kept him in the dark. The lawyer was doing the same thing, too, keeping him subordinated, using lawyerly words to confuse him. The lawyer's letter about his father's estate, the surprisingly small amount—six stores!—due to debts and bad investments. Just like his father to make *bad investments*. More facades to erect, and still being built even after the old man's sputtering demise, facades propped up for everyone but him and Beverly and that lawyer. Oh, yes, Bevy dear seemed to have gotten her fair share, which he'd deduced by simply dividing the estate's—if it could even be called such a term—worth. Maybe there would be more, hidden funds, pots of gold. Around money, how could a lawyer be trusted? *Busted*, not trusted. Erased? Anyway, there would be enough cash for a new car, a *gift* from Daddy. Yet another façade. And probably the letter was wrong, there had to be more. Six stores! All those employees, *ex-employees*.

During his last office hour of the day, Digger tended to follow the advice of the impatient right clock tower, and he did so again, locking his office door, which had once been Tobias Mann's. He pictured his old colleague seated in there, seeing only his back, for Tobias had placed his desk right before the window, his backside to the door, thus dissuading visitors. *But leading to his death, too*, thought Digger. As he turned from this image, his eyes passed by the pale square that once was the Dream Board, taken by the past, just like Tobias, and then Diana Pell, too, her slow-yet-wonderful smile. Her old office was now Lou's, Lou Knightly. Digger had still not met Angela, but he and Anna would invite them for dinner this summer. Definitely, just as soon as Anna got strong enough. Company took some strength! Digger moved up the hallway, thinking of the people who sat in those offices or who *had*, and when he got to the adjuncts' office, a flood of faces flashed by, most prominently Bill Jacobs and then Dan Pinsky's, the janitor who so loved the Lord. Maybe that was fortuitous. Digger hoped so.

And indeed he soon discovered that he was *not alone*, for partway down the History hallway worked George North, the student who didn't graduate but who stayed nonetheless. He felt a wave of camaraderie for George, but perhaps it was just a brush of empathy. Digger understood being alone in this building.

When the mopping man noticed Digger, he took off his headphones and nodded. Digger could hear a melody but couldn't tell what it was.

"What are you listening to, George?" he said.

"Metallica; do you know them?"

"Sure," said Digger, adding, "I love 'Nothing Else Matters' and that other one, the even better song, oh, yeah, 'Unforgiven.'"

"That's what I'm listening to right now," smiled George North. Digger could see the missing tooth, and he thought of the stereotype of janitors and missing teeth, janitors and alcohol, old bitter men. Unforgiven men.

Digger recited a line or two: "All I've felt, all I've known, never shined through in what I've shown."

Then George took over: "Never free, never me. Never... never ..." He couldn't remember the rest even though he'd just heard it.

"Good stuff," said Digger, who was no longer haunted by the word 'free,' Anna's old word from another life. Reborn Anna, and he'd been reborn, too. They both had been reborn twice! How many lives could a man have? Digger felt the spring semester ending right here, alone in the hallway with

George North, and it was just a little sad but mostly good, a feeling of space in time coming, one of the only times when Time itself was not an enemy. Digger began to turn away.

"Professor," said the man holding the mop, upright, as though it were a spear. "You once said that Time was Man's greatest enemy, his only enemy, do you remember that?"

"George," said Digger, "I said lots of things I don't remember!" He smiled.

"Well, I think you were right, but wrong, too. I think you can beat Time; you can win, but to win you have to act. The only way to win is to take action."

"You know what I think now, George. To beat Time you have to love. If you find love, then you can win." When the other man failed to respond, in either agreement or debate, Digger wished him a happy summer and moved down the stairs, expecting with each step to hear some words tossed in disagreement, but none came. The spring semester was ending in silence.

Out on the back path at Breezy Seas, Digger spotted a handful of robins, each patrolling an area, and he playfully pointed them out to Anna, who'd always been a bit fearful of those birds and who was now walking almost normally, with just a cane due to her leg muscles still being a bit weak. The robins darted around the grass along the pathway, looking angry and a bit resentful, as though Digger had hidden their worms. He could understand his wife's apprehension. "The robins are just waiting for you to slip up and fall, Anna." Digger giggled at that.

"Thanks for that image," said Anna, smiling, but then she said, "Maybe we should go inside after all!" Digger giggled again.

"Forget the robins, Anna. Look at that phlox!" The colorful ground cover grew wild behind the nursing home, lavender star clusters spread out above the lawn, creating a beautiful border into the small wooded area.

Anna hesitated, no doubt still eying the lurching birds. "It's pretty, but I like the dark-purple phlox even better, and the pink flowers, too. We should get all three types, Matt, and plant them out back, maybe near Snodo's grave, Snodo's and Simba's."

"That's a good idea, but we'd need to add some better soil, probably. Just too much sand out there, maybe too much wind, too. I've never had any luck with flowers."

"Have you ever planted any?"

Digger laughed, realizing that he never had. "I'll bathe you in phlox, Anna, dear," he said, and then, "Look at that robin. He's giving you the eye."

They returned to her room, Digger laughing on the way.

In the Ward C corridor, Nurse Addie said, "Here's my patient, but not for much longer. Tomorrow, right? You've gotten your walking papers."

"Tomorrow!" said Anna, adding, "Then I have to eat this guy's food. I think I'll miss the meals at Breezy Seas."

Nurse Addie smiled and said that Anna could come back at any time. She made a face at Digger, but then she said that he could come back, too. "You two are my favorite success stories," she said. "Most patients don't leave this ward the way you two have, on your feet. Why, one poor fellow was even murdered, if you could believe what the police said or at least thought, with all the *interrogations* we had to go through. Do you remember that, from last fall, long before you came here, Anna? Do you remember George North?"

Digger had been smiling but only half listening, thinking mainly of 'tomorrow,' but at the name, he opened his eyes and ears wide. "Did you say 'George North'? How do you know George North?"

"That was the name of the man who died with cookies or crackers or something in his throat, the one who suffocated but whose monitor had been unplugged. George North. He wasn't even an old man, not really. Last fall, it was in the news. The man who died here."

In that moment, the year's events started to come together, the puzzle pieces forming. George North *Senior*, how could that be a coincidence? None of those existed, right, Detective Doyle? Just villains and repetition.

"Anna, Nurse Addie, I've got to go. I'll see you later this afternoon. I've got to see about something. I'll feed Bumper, too," he added, in order to make the moment seem more normal. But his heart was racing, and a cold baseball was forming in his gut, moving slowly upwards. He kissed Anna, but the icy ball continued to rise.

Digger hardly concentrated on the drive home. He thought of George's negative comments about his father and about the senior's murder, for who else could it have been? Were there actually two George North's? Not possible, but he'd find out. Back to the Yellow Pages, that's where Digger would get his final answers. George had worked at OVC for a decade, at least, so his name and number would no doubt be in the phone book, as would an old man's. Would Digger find two Norths, both Georges? If so, then the former student would be off the hook, *but if not?* Then Digger would drive to the listed address and look for a blue Hyundai Elantra, *and if he found it?* Then George North would die.

Although the Ocean View Yellow Pages included both Bayside and Middleburg, the book itself was fairly small, the white pages up front, then the yellow businesses behind. Digger broke the white pages in the middle and almost immediately landed in the N's, first on a 'Norris,' then on a group of 'Norton's,' then smack in the middle on a single 'North.' Then he couldn't remember why finding two would mean less than one? Couldn't the father have lived further away, outside this phone book's area? He just couldn't remember his reasoning, yet he knew with crystal clarity what he had to do: drive to 431 Parkside Avenue in Middleburg and find a blue Elantra with dents.

As a distraction while driving, Digger turned the radio to one of only two remaining classic rock stations and turned up the volume. Within fifteen minutes and three songs, two by Led Zeppelin, Digger discovered that while 'Parkside Avenue' sounded like a main road, it was hardly bigger than Cottage View, but that's where the two locals parted ways. Parkside must have housed ten times the number of people, for every other 'house' was an apartment complex, most with two levels, and number 431 turned out to be an especially large building. It needed a new coat of white paint and definitely some landscaping. The few trees looked like maples, but the branches were grey, not red tipped. Nothing blossomed easily on Parkside Avenue. The phone book hadn't mentioned an apartment number, but Digger didn't need one. He just drove through the front parking lot to the back, which was bigger. He saw many dark blue cars, a couple of light blue ones, and one robin's egg pickup truck. *No Elantra.* Then he saw a vehicle covered over by the big garbage receptacle. Beneath the off-white canvas, Digger could see a strip of blue, a sky beneath storm clouds, and his heart started to thump again.

He parked right in front of the car, as though cutting off its escape route, shut off the engine right in the middle of "Bohemian Rhapsody," something he'd never done to that song before, and approached the hidden car, somewhat hesitantly because the cold baseball had moved into his throat and made it hard to breathe. Bending, he lifted the tarp a foot and read the blue car's license plate: BB9112. *Bilbo Baggins and the Devil!* Matthew Diggerson gulped at the air and then lifted the cover even more. He saw the drunk looking 'H' that signified Hyundai, not Honda, and then he moved to the back of the car, pulled up the grubby cover, and saw 'Elantra.' And dents, dents on the front, the back, and even one side, as though the driver had gotten into a variety of accidents, and that word, 'accident,' made Digger's head expand. He wondered if the bullet would explode, and that thought actually calmed him down. He had to be calm. He had to think.

This was George North's car, *had to be.* It was his address, and even though the apartment complex must hold hundreds of people, how could he have hunted the janitor to this address and not found *his* car. His *hidden* car. He must be driving another one, and that's why Digger hadn't been able to find the Elantra since Spring Break. *Since Jolie's murder.*

Was George 'home' now? Was he looking out a window at this very moment? Digger scanned the long apartment complex, the first and second floor windows, and saw nobody, but he could still be there, just standing back from any of the windows, away from the light. Should he go to the cops? What would they do? Would they come out and inspect the Hyundai? If so, they'd find something, had to. The car couldn't crush Jolie and not have any forensics. Poor Jolie! This car had done it, George North had done it. Killed Jolie and tried to kill Anna. Why Anna? Because of him, because of Matthew Diggerson, but why? He'd always been nice to George, respectful, why not? Hadn't George himself said that Digger was the *only one* to talk with him? The man would have to be a nut to kill friends. *Friends?* Digger thought of Detective Doyle's words about 'family.' How could a person ever be totally understood? George had killed his father, in cold blood at Breezy Seas, so whatever problems he'd had been nourished into his roots. His mother had mentioned those once, something about 'roots being deep,' so George's problems had incubated for decades. *Somewhat like Eliot Gladstone,* thought Digger. George was just another Eliot.

Just as he'd decided, tentatively, to use Anna's cell phone to call Detective Busher (or any cop, for that matter), a black Corolla pulled into the back lot and stopped near Digger's black Yaris. *Both in the Toyota family*, thought Digger absurdly, and then he recognized the face behind the slightly tinted windows. *George Frackin' North!*

George cranked down the window, his face much paler now, and he smiled. "I see you found my old car, Professor. You really are quite the sleuth, just like in your books."

Digger took a step toward the Corolla, toward George, but the space between them seemed thick, like an invisible shield. Digger was gulping for air again.

"Got something in your throat, Professor. My old man had that problem! Now he doesn't, though." George laughed, and through the haze, Digger saw the missing tooth, two of them, little holes in the man's grin. George stopped smiling and said, "Gotta go, Professor. What do you say you chase me? A race! Best man wins!"

Then George slowly rolled the tinted window back up, the shadow rising to cover the killer's face, and when the Corolla started to move away, Digger was finally released. He engulfed a breath and yanked open his car door, glanced to see where George had gotten to (almost out of the back lot), twisted the car's ignition, swung the Yaris around as though it were a racecar, and roared after his foe, who'd disappeared toward Parkside Avenue.

Digger heard a booming sound and realized that it was his radio, which he'd never switched off. The strident strumming of electric guitars, the notes caressing his emotions and giving them strength. Digger suddenly recognized the haunting beginning sounds of "Creep" by Radiohead. The vocals were about to start. *Pay attention*, Digger ordered himself. No cars appeared on Parkside, but Digger had to look both ways for George anyway, and he spotted him going left, toward OVC, so he pushed the pedal down and gave chase, got going amazingly fast in just a few seconds, way too fast for the little road, but Digger didn't care. All that mattered was speed and catching George and maybe slamming into him and then throttling the bastard. Anna's attacker, Jolie's killer, that's who Digger thought of, but mainly Anna, over and over of Anna, and as he chased after George North, Radiohead blared, and Matthew Diggerson joined the group, bellowed "Creep!" along with the main singer and then repeated that word on his own, 'Creep, Creep, Creep, Creep,' driving like he was out in the Four Corners region of the southwest with nothing passing by but buttes and cacti. With the song blaring and the speed, Digger seemed thrust into a film thriller, a fictional life, but what was odd about that? Who else but Diggerson had his home invaded by deranged men with knives and guns? Who else had colleagues stabbed and throttled and thrown down stairs? Who else had a spouse run over by a car? Who else but Matthew Frackin' Diggerson!

"I'm a creep!" sang Radiohead, and "You're a creep!" bellowed the writing instructor, and the back-road chase went left and right and left. Digger had no idea where he was and didn't care at all, but then he recognized the main strip leading to OVC. Was George going 'home'? What was his end plan? But Digger mainly had nothing in his head but revenge and the pounding melody and vocals to "Creep."

"You don't belong here!" Digger screamed with the song, over and over, and George seemed to hear him because Digger saw the janitor's eyes in the man's rearview mirror, wide and white, prey without a prayer, and hadn't he once seen eyes like that on the approaching Bay Bridge? Digger blotted out that memory by yelling "You're a creep! You don't belong here!" And then the chase headed toward the sky, right up the Bye Bye Bridge.

Digger thought of Paul Smith, who'd tried to kill him, and then of Eliot Gladstone, who'd come very close to killing him, twice at least, and now he *was* them. Now *he* was the killer, the predator, the pursuer, but George North wouldn't emerge as Digger had, better off every time, more alive, grateful. No, George would just come out of this *dead*.

Diggerson looked insane, his eyes wide and piercing blue. What a *nut!* What a crazy race, but either way, with his victory or with Diggerson's, there would be no more mopping. The cat was out of the bag, unless Diggerson could be eliminated, erased, and under the present circumstances, that didn't look too promising. For a moment, George pictured himself rising into the sky, but then he realized that he was just cresting the Bay Bridge, that he was on top of the world, that Diggerson wouldn't give up, and that now he was going down. His new old car was performing well, though. The two grand had been a deal, despite the lack of hubcaps. Why did old Corollas always have missing hubcaps? And why were new ones so damn expensive, more so than headlights even? George decided that if he made it out of this chase alive and free, he'd paint his rims to cover the lack of hubcaps. Blue would go well with the black.

Then he had to concentrate better. Faster and faster, unbelievably fast, he was descending, and all that was coming was *trees, trees, trees*, but if he could just take that left turn, then Diggerson would see those big pines, too, see them right up close, right into his stupid, blue-eyed face, but the turn was too sharp, *oh!*

The used Corolla left the road, leaped the guard rails, and sailed through the air, absolutely flew, like a car in the movies, and George North, the one-time student, the one-time son, the friend to a few, the eternal janitor, he left the earth and thought, "Mom! I'm flying, flying!" and then one last thought, a millisecond's worth of statement, "I'm coming."

Up and over the bridge, Digger pursued George North with a sort of reckless glee, a careless joy, and in his mind his little car became a weapon that would take the janitor out, somewhere down there in Bayside. He had gained on Anna's

would-be killer, and again he saw his former student's eyes in
the rearview mirror, through the tinting even, big eyes, lots of
white, round, terrified looking (or maybe just excited), and
Digger had seen eyes like that before, and this time he allowed
himself to picture Danny Jones' saucer-shaped orbs as the boy
clung like a sad little thing to the bridge pylon all those years
ago, and all at once Digger lost his fire and took his foot off the
accelerator. George's car began to widen the gulf between them
and to recede down the steep slope of the bridge's far side. Too
steep, too fast, and Digger remembered that the road swung left
at its base, and in that instant he realized that physics wouldn't
allow a car moving with so much force to make that turn, and
then the black Corolla with the tinted windows was in the air,
aloft like a hunted rabbit in mid hop, and before it landed back
on earth, the vehicle collided with one of the old sentinel pines
that lined both sides of the Bay Bridge. With his windows up,
the water's winds pressing in, and especially the crackling of
adrenalin in his ears, Digger heard no impact but saw George's
car disappear into the tree's broad base, like an accordion, the
front stopped but the back continuing, and Digger thought of
Tolkien's orc who'd killed Boromir and who then pulled
Aragorn's sword through its own body to reach his foe, for
George's car just kept going in, and now it was just a cube, a
flattened black can of Coke Zero, and it fell from the trunk into
the shadows beneath the quivering giant of a pine. And like the
orc, the great tree couldn't live with all that ingested metal, for
it swayed forward, lurched back, and snapped, disappearing
into the thin arms of its brothers, who could not prevent its fall.
Who could?

Digger took the left turn at a normal speed, noting that
nobody was coming up behind him, nobody in front, either, and

that he'd been the only witness to George North's sudden exit from this world. He expected to see a fireball, at the very least some flames, but nothing but a snapped off broad tree trunk was immediately visible to any passersby.

The professor progressed up the road, feeling tired suddenly, and as he turned off his radio, Digger wondered about himself. He'd just caused another man's death, that was the truth, couldn't be denied, and he'd wanted that death. He'd bellowed like a wild man, and George was now dead. Was Digger happy? Sad, guilty, frightened? He had to admit that he didn't feel much at all. He pulled off the road at Mario's Pizza, but not to eat, just to think. What would the police do with this new information, once George's car was found? Another link from a car 'accident' to OVC, to the FOB specifically, the actual Faculty Office Building, just across the water, and when the latest 'victim' was connected to the blue Elantra out hidden in his parking lot off Parkside Avenue, to the BB9112 license plate that Digger had given to Detective Busher (if the cop had even written it down), what would the authorities do then? Should Digger call the police, report the accident, fess up to his role in it?

He looked both ways and then drove toward the bridge, slowly but not strangely so, and when he passed the crash site, he could see nothing, just the broken tree and the shadows below, so he headed up the bridge. He had become Billy D Wilder, his own hero. Like the surviving cowboy in an old western, the villain lying vanquished in the dusty street, Digger was riding away into the sunset, the credits rolling. All he needed was a saloon and a host of awestruck townspeople in place of the pine trees and bridge pylons. In half a minute, he'd reached the apex and then disappeared.

Matthew Diggerson remembered his own mad escape from Breezy Seas one autumn night nearly a decade ago, but this one was even better. Sanctioned by the staff, too. And after a rainy May night, the morning dawned bright and spoke only of spring, of rebirth. Digger had asked Anna if she wanted him to get the car and pick her up at the front door, like a celebrity, but she'd chosen to walk. "I'm leaving *with* you," she had just said. "Just like we did that night long ago, Matt. Remember your 'escape'?" He did. He smiled. He giggled. Round and round.

Then Digger laughed again, for on the sidewalk ahead he'd spotted an earthworm, wagging its cranium about (or tail?) but not really going anywhere, not fast enough, anyway. "Look," he said to Anna, pointing. "Nature can be cruel."

Anna laughed, leaned even more into his side, and said, "Don't say anything about a 'face'!" Digger giggled again.

They stopped before the little animal, what Digger sometimes called 'nature's pasta,' and he bent down to scoop it up and toss the earthworm beneath a bush along the sidewalk. "He should be okay in there." said Digger, and Anna responded, "Or 'she'."

"Worms are even harder to figure out than cats," said Digger, wiping his hand against his Anna-less side, and then the two continued on their path, heading for the future.

From the doorway, the quiet aide watched the couple moving away from Breezy Seas, from her. It was beautiful to see how he buoyed her, how she hung on him against the spinning of the earth, how the sun shone down between the white clouds, the birds zigzagging through the blue sky and green trees, the dew glistening on the grass. It was all so beautiful. "O-oh-o!" said Ana Cepatos.

ABOUT THE AUTHOR

 After graduating from the University of Connecticut and then the University of Arizona, Dave Gillespie returned to New England to teach college composition and continues to do so. In Providence, Rhode Island, he lives happily with his wife (Elena), who helps him to revise and proofread his stories, and one remaining dog (Holly). His "Simba" (named Sweetie) passed away peacefully in 2013 at the age of 16, and one inspiration for "Snodo" (Belle) just left the earth in February of 2020 at 17 plus years of age. They are missed.

Ominous Outcomes is the fifth in his Matthew Diggerson mysteries. The first four were *Rules to Die By, Planning to Die, Marked For Murder,* and *The Dart of Persuasion.*